"Do that again," she breathed joyfully.

He lifted her off her feet this time, his mouth hot and wet, moving across hers as if he were devouring a feast. "What have you done to me?" he murmured, an almost desperate note in his voice.

"I was about to ask you the same." She plunged her hands into his thick, dark hair and tugged. "Kiss me again. Please."

His hand slid down to her buttocks, lifting her tighter against his unmistakable reaction to her. She groaned, crawling even closer to him if possible, all but purring her pleasure. Her hands crept around his ribs to his back, kneading rigid muscles...and encountering something wet.

He hissed into her mouth and lurched upright, arching his back away from her.

"What did I do?" she asked quickly, in distress.

"It's my back. Some nutcase tried to stab you a few minutes ago and sliced me instead."

"Stab—me?" And then the rest of it hit her. "You've been *stabbed?*"

Dear Reader,

Let's extend our summer lovin' with this month's Silhouette Romantic Suspense offerings. Reader-favorite Kathleen Creighton will enthrall you with *Daredevil's Run* (#1523), the latest in her miniseries THE TAKEN. Here, an embittered man reunites with his long-lost love as they go on a death-defying adventure in the wilderness. You'll feel the heat from Cindy Dees's *Killer Affair* (#1524), the third book in SEDUCTION SUMMER. In this series, a serial killer murders amorous couples on the beach, and no lover is safe. Don't miss the exciting conclusion to this sizzling roller-coaster ride!

When a handsome hero receives a mysterious postcard, he joins forces to find its sender with the woman who secretly loves him. Can they overcome a shared tragedy and face the future together? Find out in Justine Davis's emotional tale *Her Best Friend's Husband* (#1525), which is part of her popular REDSTONE, INCORPORATED miniseries. Finally, let's give a big welcome to Jennifer Morey, who debuts in the line with *The Secret Soldier* (#1526), and begins her miniseries ALL McQUEEN'S MEN. In this action-packed story, a dangerous—and ultrasexy—military man must rescue a kidnapped scientist. As they risk life and limb, they discover an unforgettable chemistry.

This month, you'll find love against the odds and adventures lurking around every corner. Enjoy these gems from Silhouette Romantic Suspense!

Sincerely,

Patience Smith
Senior Editor

Killer
AFFAIR

Cindy Dees

Silhouette®

Romantic

SUSPENSE

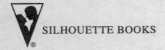

SILHOUETTE BOOKS

ISBN-13: 978-0-373-27594-6
ISBN-10:   0-373-27594-3

KILLER AFFAIR

CINDY DEES

started flying airplanes while sitting in her dad's lap at the age of three, and got a pilot's license before she got a driver's license. At age fifteen, she dropped out of high school and left the horse farm in Michigan where she grew up to attend the University of Michigan. After earning a degree in Russian and East European Studies, she joined the U.S. Air Force and became the youngest female pilot in the history of the Air Force. She flew supersonic jets, VIP airlift and the C-5 Galaxy, the world's largest airplane. She also worked part-time gathering intelligence. During her military career, she traveled to forty countries on five continents, was detained by the KGB and East German secret police, got shot at, flew in the first Gulf War, met her husband and amassed a lifetime's worth of war stories.

Her hobbies include professional Middle Eastern dancing, Japanese gardening and medieval reenacting. She started writing on a one-dollar bet with her mother and was thrilled to win that bet with the publication of her first book in 2001. She loves to hear from readers and can be contacted at www.cindydees.com.

This one wouldn't have been possible without Nina, Sheree and Tashya. Thanks, ladies, for the inspiration, laughter and sand between my toes when I needed them.

Chapter 1

Another gust flung the tiny airplane sideways like a storm-tossed cork. Tom Laruso's formidable muscles strained as he fought the controls, leveling out the Cessna floatplane's wings and easing it down toward a lower and hopefully smoother altitude.

"Are we going to die?" the woman beside him quavered.

"Nah. This is just a little turbulence. No big deal. Think of it as a giant roller coaster. Take my advice, little lady, just sit back and enjoy the ride."

She subsided, white-knuckled, beside him. Didn't look as if she was buying the roller-coaster line. She'd been insane to insist on this trip, and he'd told her as much before they left the big island. But the client, who'd called herself only Madeline C., had been adamant. She had to get to Vanua Taru *tonight*. Hey, if she had a death wish, who was he to stand in her way? It wasn't like staying alive held any great appeal to him. He was game to dance with death if she was.

But now that they were out here flirting with the leading edge of a Category Three hurricane—cyclones, they were called out here in the South Pacific—he wasn't so sure this was the way he wanted to go. He'd much rather lose himself in the bottom of a whiskey bottle and just drift away, numb and painless.

The plane lurched, its left wing jerking up suddenly and half flinging him into Ms. Madeline's elegant lap. His right hand gripped her thigh, which went as rock hard beneath his palm as any self-respecting stair-climber queen's. He murmured an apology and pushed himself upright. His biceps strained as he wrestled with the yoke and finally bullied the plane back into more or less level flight.

She *would* have to look just like Arielle. Tom glanced over briefly at his passenger in the waning dusk. Hell, she even smelled like Arielle, all light and floral like some damned butterfly. It was uncanny, actually. The fine bones, silver-blond halo of hair, the dreamy, mint-green eyes. How many women anywhere looked like that? And to have two so similar come into his life one right after another… Yup. Weird. If Arielle was haunting him, he'd kill her…oh, wait. She was already dead. Searing guilt twisted in his gut. God, he needed a drink.

Something flashed at the edge of his vision, a streak of light, falling from above and slashing through the arc of the propeller. The plane bucked. The engine hitched and coughed. Not good. Instinctively, he pushed the yoke forward, putting the plane into a descent. When in doubt, get out of the sky and land. Or in this case, float. Miles and miles of ocean stretched away in every direction. All the landing zone a guy could ever ask for. Even if it was heaving into massive mountains and valleys of salt water as the cyclone approached.

He started to glance down at the engine gauges to see if any caution lights had illuminated on the master warning panel, when another flash of white light streaked past his peripheral vision. Crap. Another lightning strike.

He had no more time to think on the possible implications of the strike as flames erupted from the engine cowling directly in front of him. His passenger screamed. Immediately he shoved the nose over as hard as it would go. They had to get down!

The steep dive blew out some of the fire, but it was coming out the other side of the engine, if the woman's continued screams were any indication. No time to reassure her, though. Not as if he had any comforting words for her, anyway. They were in a world of hurt. He fought the jerking plane grimly. The wild aluminum bronco was winning. This wasn't turbulence. Something was terribly wrong. The propeller wobbled, horribly unbalanced, all but shaking the little plane apart.

The ocean loomed near. He literally stood on the rudder pedals and hauled back on the yoke for all he was worth. The Cessna groaned its protest, metal creaking and wing spars shuddering under the strain of the g-forces he was violently overloading them with.

C'mon, baby, hang together just a few more seconds. Every muscle in his body strained, pushed to the limit to maintain control of the aircraft. Were he not as strong a man as he was, they'd already be spiraling out of control into the sea.

Something tore off the nose of the plane and flew back, slamming into the windshield directly in front of him. The Plexiglas cracked into a crazed spiderweb that completely blocked his vision of the angry mountains of water just below.

He shouted at his passenger, "We've got to bail out! Open your door and jump! It's not far to the water!"

He glanced over only to see her face contorted into a soundless scream of terror. She'd frozen on him. He let go of his own door handle to reach across her and push her door open. He shoved her toward the yawning void.

And then the plane exploded.

The burst of light and heat was blinding, like being consumed by the sun. He registered a vague sensation of the Cessna evaporating around him, flying outward until nothing remained but fire and the deafening roar of it. He floated weightless for a millisecond, then the explosion slammed into him in all its fury.

The world went black.

Madeline hit the water feetfirst, stunned by how much the impact hurt and how *cold* the ocean was. It shocked her horrified mind into a moment of utter, frozen panic, but then the icy chill penetrated and jolted her back to full awareness.

The great pressure of water all around her was terrifying. She opened her eyes, squinting against the violent sting of salt. But there was faint light above. She swam for it, her lungs burning. Her arms and legs were unbearably heavy, and she fought for all she was worth toward that flickering beacon of life.

It must have been only a few seconds, but each arm stroke, each desperate kick, each sluggish lurch toward the surface seemed to take an eternity. Her lungs were ready to explode and her eyes screamed their pain, but she fought on grimly.

And then she burst through to the surface, her head and shoulders erupting from the sea's deathly embrace, breaking free to air and a deep, blessed gasp. *She was alive.*

She treaded water, turning in a slow circle to observe the debris littering the surface around her. Huge ocean swells bobbed her up and down in twilight's last light. Now what the heck was she supposed to do? Her arms and legs were tiring fast. She paddled toward the nearest floating object, a large panel of metal lined with some sort of foam. Upon closer inspection, she saw it was the backseat of the airplane, a double-wide bench affair.

Whaddiya know. Those airplane seat cushions did float after all. She grabbed it and dragged her tired body across it. And as she glanced beyond the cushion, she spied something that tore a scream out of her hoarse throat.

A man's face. Floating just below the surface of the water, pale and ghostlike, slipping away slowly into the abyss.

The pilot. Tom Something. Alicia had recommended him.

She lunged across the cushion, kicking wildly, and grabbed for him. She got a handful of his shirt. She pulled with all her might and managed to bring his face up to the surface. Lord, he was heavy. She rolled off the long cushion and wrestled awkwardly to shove it underneath the man's back. She swallowed what seemed like gallons of salt water as she flailed frantically, trying to keep herself afloat, support the pilot's dead weight and get the damned cushion under the guy. Finally, she got him draped awkwardly on his back across the cushion and situated herself in the water beside him with one arm thrown across his chest to keep him from rolling off.

Ahead, she saw a faint line of twinkling lights on the horizon. Was it land? Or was it no more than a hallucination born of her desperate desire to be safe?

She did a slow three-hundred-sixty degree turn timed with when the swells lifted her up high and saw nothing else in the descending vacuum of night. Just a long, uninterrupted line where the gray-black of the sea met the blue-black of the sky to the north and south. Far to the east, she made out flickers of distant lightning. Tropical Cyclone Kato was roaring toward them.

She'd been a fool to try to race the storm to Vanua Taru, but she'd really wanted to just get the job done and go home to safe, boring Chicago before this awful trip got any worse. One of her Secret Traveler colleagues, Zoë Conrad, had gotten involved with a resort owner accused of murder and they'd nearly died before the police figured out another man had done it. Her second colleague and good friend, Alicia Greco, had been kidnapped and nearly killed by the same murderer, a serial killer who was still at large. The way their luck had been going, she was next in line for some disaster to befall her. Apparently, trying to run away from that bad luck had led her straight into it. A plane crash of all things!

For lack of anything else to do or anywhere else to go, she aimed the pilot's limp body at the lights and started kicking. She didn't even know if he was alive or dead. But if their positions had been reversed, she'd have wanted him to take her body ashore and not leave it for the sharks and whatever else lurked beneath the sea.

How long she swam, up and down the enormous waves, on and on in a morass of fatigue and pain that clenched her entire body in its vise, she had no idea. She threw up a few times. Probably a combination of swallowed seawater and shock. She stopped to rest a couple of times, too, but each time the flashes of lightning behind her seemed closer. She had no idea how far the electrical charge of a lightning strike could travel underwater, but she bloody well didn't want to find out the hard way. She dug deep and forced herself to get moving again.

True night fell quickly, the last vestiges of daylight wiped out by the encroaching storm bands of Kato. It was unbelievably dark out here. She could barely see her own hand in front of her face. Literally. Whenever she and Tom swooped down into the bottom of a trough and the line of shore lights was blocked, it seemed as if she'd been swallowed up by the depths of hell. But then the ocean would fling them dizzyingly, frighteningly high and she'd get a quick fix on her goal before being sucked down into the belly of the beast once more.

At some point, the pilot groaned and moved a bit. He was alive, then. Her exhaustion was such that she barely had time to register exultation that she wasn't entirely alone out here in the vast ocean. She didn't even particularly like water. She'd grown up on a farm in central Illinois, about as far from oceans as it got.

But in a flash, the Pacific Ocean had become her entire world, her entire existence. Just her and the cold, seductive embrace of the sea, slowly, inexorably sucking the life out of her. Well, the unconscious pilot was here, too. But at the moment, he was still little more than deadweight.

With dogged determination, fighting for both of their lives, she plowed on, pitting her tiny will against the massive expanse of ocean all around her.

That line of lights might possibly be drawing a little closer, but it could also totally be her imagination. And then, all of a sudden, she became aware of a black silhouette on the horizon. A jagged hump above the line of lights. *Land.*

Relief coursed through her, making her limbs warm and weak. Not far, now. She became aware that she was sobbing, breathing in ineffective gasps, but she didn't care. *Almost there. Almost safe.* With renewed strength, she swam on, using her free arm to paddle while she kicked the fiery spaghetti that was her legs.

Finally, she heard waves breaking nearby and smelled the

green, living scent of land. She was close to shore now. Some-thing banged into her foot, startling her. It was rough. Oh, God. Was that a shark? To be this close to land and be attacked now....

She kicked furiously. Again, something banged into her feet, hard.

Then enlightenment broke across her mind. That was *sand* dragging against her toes! She tried to stand up, but the bottom past the sandbar was still a bit too deep. She paddled on a few more yards and was able to stand up between waves this time, her chin barely out of the water. She pushed off the bottom and swam a little more. In a few seconds, she was able to walk between sets of waves. When the breakers weren't rolling in, the water was no more than chest-deep. But when the angry surf caught them up and flung them forward, she guessed the water was ten-feet deep beneath them.

The good news was the waves pushed the pilot's makeshift raft shoreward in front of her. The even better news was a sandy beach stretched before them. They wouldn't be dashed to death against rocks tonight. A violent undertow of waves rushing back out to sea sucked at her legs and lower torso. It was all she could do to hang on to Tom's raft and ride the surface waves to shore.

But then she could stand up, no more than thigh-deep. Even when a big wave came in, she was able to jump into it and land mostly back on her feet. She dragged Tom the last few feet to shore on his floating pallet. Without the sea's buoyancy to hold him, he abruptly was unbelievably heavy. But she had to get him far enough out of the water so he wouldn't drown.

Using the piece of metal backing still attached to the cushion as a sort of sled, she dug in her heels and leaned back, pulling on his inert form with all her strength. By inches, she managed to wrestle him up the beach to what seemed a safe distance from the water.

They'd made it.

Relief making her even shakier than she already was, she knelt down on her hands and knees to check him for injuries. Not that there was a whole lot she could do about it even if she had found something wrong with him, but it seemed like the thing to do. She ran her hands over his bare legs…they were muscular and hard. Under the tattered remnants of his short-sleeved shirt, the guy had an impressive set of shoulders. She didn't find any obvious broken bones or cuts.

The guy sure was in great shape—and shaped great. Were she not so exhausted, hardly able to keep her eyes open, she'd have enjoyed drinking her fill of the sight of him. As it was, a thrill of…something…tingled through her palms and throughout her body at touching him like this. It was terribly personal. So…intimate.

Despite getting felt up by her, he remained unconscious. A head injury, maybe? She pressed her ear to his chest to listen to his heart, and its beat was a slow, steady thump beneath her ear. Stymied as to what to do for him, her own exhaustion finally overcame her. Shivering, she stretched out on the warm sand beside him, pressing the length of her body against his solid, reassuring heat. Mmm. Nice. She laid her head on his shoulder. Whether she passed out or merely fell asleep she couldn't say as the darkness closed in around her, sucking her down, down, into nothingness.

Tom roused slowly. His first sensation was of a splitting headache. And then pain. Grinding slowly through his entire body. He must've gone on a hell of a bender to feel this bad. He was wet. And lying in sand. He struggled to sort through the fog enveloping him. Something heavy was sprawled across him.

And that something was soft. Curvy. Intensely feminine. *Hello.* He made a habit of never picking up women when he went on a binge. He hated not remembering anything about them the morning after, not their name, nor where he'd met them or even what they'd done together. But apparently he'd broken his rule.

He lifted his impossibly heavy arm and looped it around the woman's tiny waist. Her toes tickled his shins, and her head rested on his shoulder. She felt small against him. Fragile. That was odd. He never went for the petite, delicate ones. They usually made him feel big and awkward and clumsy.

He cracked one eye open. The sky overhead was black. Turbulent. Looked like bad weather brewing. Groggy recollection swam through his head, half-understood. Something about a storm coming.

His brain might not be working, but his ears were. A sound not of the night registered. The ocean was rumbling like a ticked-off Rottweiler to his left. But this noise came from his right. From the shoreside. A rhythmic whoosh of sand, too slow for someone walking at normal speed. But if that person were creeping cautiously toward a threat of some kind, the measured noises were about right.

Instinct roared through him. *Danger!*

The man crouched in the shadows, stunned. He couldn't believe what he was seeing! After all the publicity, all the news coverage, this pair in front of him had the temerity to roll around like a couple of savages on a beach?

For the past few weeks—ever since the last cleansing of souls he'd undertaken—the beaches he prowled had been satisfyingly deserted. Pure. This part of the world was unbelievably sinful. Tucked far away from most of the world, the South Pacific attracted people who wanted to hide their dirty affairs.

The woman in front of him moved, draping herself even more blatantly across her lover. Rage exploded behind his eyes, sending ice picks of unbearable agony through his skull. He grabbed his head with both hands to keep it from splitting in two.

Must. Stop. The. Pain.

He fumbled at his waist blindly, feeling for God's instrument of punishment. His palm caressed the form-fitted rubber grip, his loyal and trusty friend. His vision cleared, and the sinners—all but naked—writhed before him.

Usually, he waited until they were lost in the throes of their sin, but these two were taking too long, and the pain in his head…ah, God, the pain…he couldn't take it anymore….

He moved farther out of the shadow of the trees, one cautious step at a time.

Tom struggled to rip away the gauze obscuring his brain, to bring himself to full battle alert. But his head wouldn't cooperate. And his body responded even more sluggishly. He flailed against the awful feeling of paralysis gripping him.

Threat! He didn't question the intuition. It had saved his neck and his clients' more times than he could count. If only his body and mind would obey him…he silently cursed himself.

With effort, he managed to slit his right eye open enough to make out a pale ankle protruding from a khaki pant leg. It was hairy. Male, then. Caucasian. Easing forward, rolling from heel to toe with each careful step, like a hunter stalking his prey.

The screaming voice of caution in Tom's head was deafening. *Trouble! Warning! Wake up!* But still, his mind and body steadfastly refused to answer the call. He felt drugged, unable to swim free of the haze of it.

The feet stopped maybe six feet away.

Below the crashing noise of the sea, a male voice muttered something just beyond the edge of Tom's hearing, syllables that didn't quite form meaning in his sluggish mind. But the tone of voice was unmistakably hostile, dripping in vitriol.

Tom forcibly readied himself for action, ordering his muscles into a state of relaxed readiness. He was probably deluding himself that they would react with any semblance of speed or accuracy to his commands. But his threat-response training had been drilled into him so deeply over the years that even now, barely conscious, mind and body went through the motions.

The woman, perhaps because of his arm tightening about her waist, moved against him, a sinuous, sexy stretch across his sprawled body that would have riveted him had it not been for those feet paused in the sand so close.

"Whore," the voice gritted out. "Sinners."

Blank incomprehension was all Tom's mind could muster to the unexpected words. But as he regained his senses bit by bit, he became aware of evil radiating from the stranger. Malice rolled off the man in waves as every bit as powerful as the ocean's fury beside them.

The guy leaped.

In sheer reflex, Tom exploded into motion, rolling away from the pouncing attack, carrying the girl with him, covering her protectively with his body, presenting his back to the attacker. Something slashed past him, burying itself in the sand where they'd been lying, not a second before. Agonizing pain sliced across his back. His skin melted like butter before a hot knife. *A knife.* The bastard had just cut him!

Tom surged up onto his hands and knees, driven by the pain, some primitive part of his brain taking over completely. On pure instinct, he leaped to his feet and whirled, dropping low into a fighting crouch, his hands outstretched before him. Killing rage roared through his brain. This wasn't fight or flight. This was kill or be killed. Fury erupted from his throat in a feral snarl.

The attacker was already running, a dark shadow fleeing up the beach and melting into the jungle beyond. Tom lunged forward, intent on catching his prey and crushing him, when a mewl of distress from behind drew him up short.

The woman.

Reluctantly, he turned away from the trees and dropped to his knees beside her. Had the bastard hurt her with that deflected knife slash?

Quick concern sent his hands skimming over her baby-soft skin. No dark welling of blood marred her body anywhere. He squatted on his heels and pushed her wet, stringy hair away from her face.

His mind stumbled. Arielle? No, not Arielle. Not even asleep had *she* ever looked this sweet. This angelic. Who was this woman he'd apparently picked up and made love to on the beach, if her mostly unclothed state was any indication?

He plucked at the scrap of cloth clinging to her slender shoulder. The edge of it was black. Almost charred-looking. No accounting for fashion among the jet-set party girls who came to the South Pacific to play, far from the prying eyes of the paparazzi.

A remembered flash of something black blinked past his mind's eye. Sprinkled with round shapes. He frowned. Reached for the vision again. Dials of some kind.

An airplane instrument panel. What did that have to do with anything?

The woman at his feet groaned. He ran his fingers across her forehead and down her cheek to the graceful, elegant line of her neck. She reminded him of an expensive Persian kitten. Even soaking wet and passed out cold, she was stylish. How in the hell had he landed a classy act like her? She was way out of his league these days. He had to give himself credit; he'd sure picked himself a looker. Man, the two of them must have painted the town red. He wished he remembered it.

He shrugged, and the movement sent glass-sharp daggers streaking across his back. The pain accomplished more to clear the cobwebs from his mind than anything else, so far. Tom glanced up at the jungle and then back down at the unconscious woman at his feet. They had to get out of here before that sicko came back to finish them off.

Who was that bastard, anyway? And why in the hell had he tried to stab this woman? Or maybe the guy'd been after him. Lord knew, he had plenty of enemies of his own who could account for the attack.

He reached down and scooped her up in his arms, startled at how light she was. What were the odds he could stretch their one-night stand into two? And this time he would stay stone-cold sober. He'd give his right arm to remember making love to a woman like this.

Chapter 2

A blinding flash of light, followed in a moment by a giant crack of thunder, finally roused Maddie to full consciousness. Groggily, she reminded herself that she was no longer Maddie Crummby, farm kid from central Illinois. She was Madeline C., world traveler and hotel connoisseur. At the moment, it didn't seem to really matter, though. She felt…floppy. And the universe was moving rather oddly around her.

She blinked her gritty eyes open and was startled to see a solid wall of darkly tanned skin. And muscle. Acres of it. *What the—* She jerked upright, or at least tried to. Strong arms gripped her tightly, preventing her from actually moving more than her pinkie fingers.

"Easy, kitten. I've got you."

She looked up at the deep, raspy voice. The hunky pilot who'd been flying her to Vanua Taru, who yelled at her to bail out of the airplane just before it blew up, whose life she'd saved in that interminable swim, on whose chest she'd collapsed when they finally reached shore. His name came back to her. Tom.

What a chest. Muscles rippled beautifully over it, not so thick as to be ungainly, but manly in no uncertain terms. She snuggled closer until it dawned on her what she was doing. She stiffened abruptly.

"You can put me down. I'm fine," she said quickly.

He let her feet slide slowly to the ground, which had the startling effect of pressing her body against his from her neck to her toes for an unforgettable instant. Heat built between them like chain lightning, flashing back and forth, faster and faster until it painted a dizzying chaos of light and heat in her eyes.

She clung to his strength, steadying herself as his hot skin scalded her palms. His dark eyes glowed down at her, the only steady reference point in her spinning world.

"Maybe I should carry you," he murmured. His arm tightened around her preparatory to picking her up once more, pulling her close against that magnificently naked chest of his again. She couldn't help it. She melted into him like warm butter soaking into fresh bread. An urge to lick his chest, to see if it was as rich and delicious as she imagined, overcame her.

She drew her tongue delicately across his skin. Salty. Warm. Smooth. Mmm. She liked that. He jolted away from her mouth, swearing.

She'd just *licked* a total stranger. What was *wrong* with her?

But then he was back, one arm around her shoulders, the other hand splayed against her lower back, pulling her against him, sending her whirling thoughts tumbling once more. Up and down, left and right, they tangled together, the same way her limbs did with his. Where he stopped and she began, she had no idea.

His mouth closed on hers, sucking the life out of her and breathing his back into her all in one devouring, devastating kiss. *Ho. Lee. Cow.* Never, ever, had she been kissed like that. She hadn't even known a kiss like that was *possible*. Stars exploded behind her eyes and unadulterated lust tore through her. She gasped at the sudden throbbing in places she'd never throbbed before. It wasn't that she didn't enjoy sex. It was just that she was…focused…when it came to sex. It was something she studied, even when she participated in it. She wanted to be good at it so when she landed the perfect husband she'd be able to please him. But this…this tore anything but wanting *more* clean out of her mind. She stretched up on her tiptoes hungrily.

"Do that again," she breathed joyfully.

He lifted her clear off her feet this time, his mouth hot and wet, moving across hers as if he was devouring a feast. "What have you done to me?" he muttered, an almost desperate note in his voice.

"I was about to ask you the same." She plunged her hands into his thick, dark hair and tugged. "Kiss me again. Please."

His hand slid down to her buttocks, lifting her tighter against his unmistakable reaction to her. She groaned, crawling even closer to him if it was possible, all but purring her pleasure. Her hands crept around his ribs to his back, kneading his ridged muscles…and encountered something wet.

He hissed into her mouth and lurched upright, arching his back away from her touch.

"What did I do?" she asked quickly in distress.

"My back. I got cut," he gritted out between clenched teeth.

"How?"

To her dismay, he released her and stepped back, frowning down at her. She felt terribly cold and alone without his arms around her.

He answered reluctantly, "Some nutcase tried to stab you a few minutes ago and sliced me instead."

"Stab—me?" And then the rest of it hit her. "You've been stabbed?" she cried. Fear ran cold in her blood, chilling her all the way through. "Let me see."

He turned to face her when she would've darted around behind him to see how badly he was hurt.

"It's just a scratch," he bit out, his gaze skimming down her body and back up again. A flash of something hot and forbidden glinted in his gaze. "Damn, you're beautiful," he murmured. "As much as I'd like to tear off the rest of your clothes and make love to you right here, we've got to get off this beach."

She glanced down at the remnants of her clothes and gasped. Scraps of sodden cloth clung to her chest enough to provide a minimum of modesty, but not much more than that. Her silk Chanel blouse, no less. It had cost her a week's pay and the neckline draped exactly perfectly. Drat. She'd loved that blouse.

The man in front of her shifted impatiently, peering suspiciously over her shoulder as if he expected the attacker to come back any second. Abruptly, the pieces fell together in her head. They'd been lying on a beach…it was nighttime… and he said that out of nowhere a stranger had tried to attack them…

She exclaimed, "I bet that was the Sex on the Beach Killer!"

"The who?" Tom responded blankly.

This guy hadn't heard about the psychopath roaming the South Pacific killing pairs of lovers on beaches? He'd have to be a complete hermit to have missed that news flash. The killer had last struck on Fiji's big island a couple of weeks back. He was due to strike again, according to Agent Griffin Malone, the FBI profiler who'd saved Alicia's life.

"The Sex on the Beach Killer," Maddie repeated. Cold chills that had nothing to do with being wet and nearly naked snaked down her spine. A psychopath had tried to kill them? A fine trembling erupted throughout her entire body.

"How—" Her voice broke. She tried again. "How did you scare him off?"

He shrugged.

"Did you get a good look at him? Police have been chasing him all over the place. No one knows what he looks like. Well, besides the fact that he's Caucasian and around six feet tall. I know that because my friend found a pair of his victims, and she got involved in the investigation and met the FBI profiler and she told me a little about the case, you know, what to look out for and…" And she was babbling. She did that when she got really nervous.

He stared down at her as if she was jabbering a foreign language at him.

She huffed, "You have heard of him, right? The guy who's been running around the South Pacific stabbing lovers on beaches while they…do the deed."

His eyebrows lifted at that, but he made no comment. Not real talkative, her handsome pilot. But, hey, the guy kissed like a god. She swayed toward him once more.

"C'mon," Tom growled. He took off striding down the beach, his long legs outdistancing her quickly.

"Wait up!" she called after him. She ran through the heavy sand, feeling as clumsy as a drunken chicken. Ugh. *Style note to self: never run on beaches.*

He stalked onward without slowing down to wait for her. Not exactly the most social guy on the planet when he didn't have his arms around her and his mouth on hers. Exasperated, she tagged along, wishing he'd slow down, but too unaccountably annoyed at her uncontrollable attraction to him to ask it of him.

Eventually, they came to a stretch of beach bordered by tall, rocky cliffs. Before long, he veered away from the water and headed for a pale shape zigzagging up the face of the black, wet rocks. Her gaze followed the jagged line upward. She spied a dark, rectangular hulk at the top of it, perched not far from the edge of the cliff.

They drew a little closer and she saw that the pale line was a set of stairs. It led to a *bure,* a traditional Fijian dwelling made of stucco, logs and thatch. The house nestled within a grove of banyans and palm trees.

"Who lives there?" she asked cautiously. The last thing they need to do was walk into the Sex on the Beach Killer's hideout.

Tom tossed over his shoulder, "The weather's about to get nasty. We need to seek shelter now."

"But—"

"Ladies first," he interrupted gently.

With a sigh, she set her feet to the long staircase. Something inside her was disappointed that they'd found civilization. For a minute there, she could've really enjoyed being stranded in a deserted paradise with a hunky pilot who made her knees weak when he kissed her.

Not that the fantasy *ought* to do a blessed thing for her, of course. Madeline C. didn't go for sand, drinking out of coconuts and building palm-frond shelters. She was a city girl all the way. She liked her plug-in creature comforts and was never caught without a makeup kit or the perfect shoes. Of course, she had neither at the moment. Her hair was a sodden mess, and her clothes were destroyed. She'd have to extract a promise out of the pilot never to reveal to anyone that he'd seen Madeline C. without her chic armor polished and firmly in place. And no cameras! If he took a picture of her looking like this, the Sex on the Beach Killer wouldn't be the worst of his worries!

The Plan. She had to stick with the Plan. Build a new life for herself firmly anchored in the bright lights and big city. Find herself the richest—and nicest, of course—guy she could find and marry him with all due haste. No way was she spending the rest of her life working her fingers to the bone through drought and freezing cold and searing heat to scrape a living out of the ground. She was absolutely not repeating her mother's mistake. No, sir. She was Madeline C.

She took a deep breath and peered upward, trying to catch a glimpse of the dwelling above her. Even if Tom did kiss better than ought to be legal, there was no room in her life for heavy panting with some beach bum bush pilot. Focus. It was all about focus. It was how she'd dragged herself out of the ocean, and it was how she would drag herself off the farm and into a new life.

She tromped up the stairs, her already exhausted legs burning fiercely. Her personal trainer back at the gym would be appalled that a simple set of stairs was doing her in like this. But hey! She'd spent a couple hours fighting the Pacific Ocean in all its fury. That had to count for something.

Man. What a day. This trip had been jinxed from the moment she and her fellow Secret Traveler reviewers left Chicago. She just wanted to get home, go to her favorite spa, get a mani-pedi, a full body wrap and a facial and forget she'd ever been to this miserable corner of the world with its cyclones and serial killers and tempting strangers.

She glanced at the ocean pounding behind her. The waves were getting bigger by the minute, swallowing a few more inches of the beach with every crash of surf upon the shore. She didn't know a whole lot about the South Seas, but common sense told her that spending the night down on the beach might not be the smartest thing in the world to try with a storm rolling in. Reluctantly, she continued up the long line of steps.

Finally, several stories above the ocean, she set foot on level ground once more. Tom took her elbow and escorted her firmly to the house's front door. He fiddled with the doorknob for a few seconds, and then the door opened under his hand. Good grief, the guy'd just broken into the place! She stared, appalled.

"Are you coming or not?" he tossed at her.

"I don't think we should just walk in there like this."

"Why the hell not?"

"Well, the owner might be scared if we barge in. What if he's got a gun?"

Tom snorted. "The owner has several guns."

Her eyebrows shot up in alarm. "How do you know that?"

He bit out, "I'm the owner."

She stared. "What?"

He glanced over at her and didn't bother to repeat himself. A girl could get tired of listening to herself talk, trying to have a conversation with this taciturn guy. She followed him inside. If she thought it was dark outside, it was inky black in here. She banged into something about knee-high and yelped.

"Stand still," he ordered.

She was more than happy to oblige. A light flared on the far side of the room as he lit a match. He held it to the wick of an old-fashioned oil lamp and put a glass globe down over the flame. A dim, but warm, glow suffused the open space.

The hard thing that had attacked her knees turned out to be a beautifully carved wooden end table.

The *bure*'s interior was bigger than she'd expected. A vaulted ceiling high overhead added to the impression, giant logs forming an inverted V of cantilevered support beams. If she wasn't mistaken, that was a thatched roof on top of the log frame. Lovely. Grass for shelter from an approaching hurricane.

Bamboo and mahogany furniture blended seamlessly with the white gauze curtains and crisp, ice-blue linen upholstery. A kitchen occupied one corner of the space, separated by a gorgeously carved mahogany breakfast bar with a pair of elegantly curved stools before it. It was a shockingly stylish room. And *he* lived here? Clearly, he'd bought the place furnished.

She glanced over and saw him standing in front of a mirror, peering over his shoulder at his reflection. Checking out his deltoids? She knew guys were vain, but sheesh!

And then she saw the dark slash across his back, about two inches below his shoulder blades. The Sex on the Beach Killer. He'd said the guy had scratched him, but the cut extended almost all the way across his back!

"Good Lord!" she exclaimed. "You call that gash a scratch? I'd hate to see your idea of a serious wound. Let me see that." She rushed over to examine the cut, which still oozed blood. "You need to see a doctor. That thing needs stitches."

"No doctor," he replied sharply.

"Why not?"

"Only medic on Vanua Taru is also the sheriff."

She didn't know which question to ask first. Why he wanted to avoid the law, or if they really were on Vanua Taru, which had been her destination this evening in the first place. Caution won out and she asked the second question, for fear of the answer to the first. "We're really on Vanua Taru?"

He nodded, his lips pressed together in a tight line.

"Are you in pain?"

He shrugged, a tense move of a single shoulder.

She knew that look. Her brothers and father used to get it when they'd been hurt but didn't want to act like sissies in front of one another. Tom was having a bout of macho maleness.

She rolled her eyes. "Well, at least let me clean that cut out. It has sand in it."

"I'll take care of it."

"You can barely see it, let alone reach it. Where's your first-aid kit?"

He scowled at her for a moment, then moved through a doorway into what looked from a glimpse like a bathroom. He came back in a moment with a big backpack crammed with a shockingly well-stocked first-aid kit. A person could practically perform surgery out of it. Growing up on a farm far from any immediate help, she and her siblings had all learned basic first aid early. It was surprising how much veterinary medicine applied to human beings in a pinch, too. She rummaged through the supplies until she found what she needed.

"Let's go into the bathroom. When I flush out that wound, it's going to make a mess."

He sighed, but did as she suggested. In the end, they both stepped into the big, Roman-tiled shower, clothes and all. He stood under the water until the sand and blood were gone, then she soaped up his back gently but thoroughly and finally he rinsed off again.

He turned to her, his hair slicked back from his strong, tanned features. He looked like a freaking cover model, even if he was white around the mouth at the moment. An errant urge to kiss away his pain washed over her. *Focus, girlfriend. The Plan.*

"Thanks," he murmured.

Butterflies leaped in her stomach and she took a step backward, her back coming up against the cool, tiled wall. He braced his left hand beside her head and smiled down at her a slow, lazy, sexy smile that promised hours and hours of mind-blowing lovemaking.

"Have you got any scratches I can clean out for you?" he drawled.

"I...I don't know."

"We'd better check. Cuts infect fast in this climate."

He plucked at the scrap of cloth clinging to her shoulder and she glanced down. Then stared down in shock. In the dim light of the oil lamp flickering on the counter outside the shower, the remnants of her silk shirt and her lace bra clung to her breasts transparently, leaving absolutely nothing to the imagination. She watched, mesmerized as his brown fingers trailed over the pale fabric, around the outside curve of her breast, then lightly along the sensitive underside of the mound. Her nipples puckered hard, standing up proudly, begging for his touch. She closed her eyes in mortification— and longing. Something warm and firm touched her temple.

His mouth. He was kissing her again. Her toes started to curl. Ohboyohboyohboy. *The... What was it that she was supposed to remember?* He straightened and she tipped her mouth up to his. In the midst of the warm spray of water, he captured her lips with his, sucking her lower lip into his mouth and laving it with his tongue.

Her hands crept up to his shoulders. Urged him closer. His arm swept around her waist, pulling her away from the wall and against his big, hard body. The shower pounded down, raining heat and steam all around them.

He sucked in a hard breath as the spray hit his back and

she lurched. *His injury.* And here she was, crawling all over a wounded man. She sagged against him in frustration, pressing her forehead against his chest for a moment before pushing herself away from him.

"Let's get you out of here and get that cut dressed and covered," she sighed.

He matched her sigh with one of his own. "But I didn't finish scrubbing your back yet."

"Next time."

"Promise there'll be a next time?"

Whoa, baby. There'd be a next time if she had anything to say about it! Belatedly, she recalled herself. Madeline C. The Plan. This man was trouble with a capital T.

They stepped out of the shower and dried themselves quickly, and Maddie—*Madeline*—then used paper towels to blot his wound dry. She couldn't bring herself to ruin one of the fluffy, snow-white Turkish towels from his linen closet. She had to give the guy credit. She would never have guessed he even *had* a linen closet, let alone one neatly stocked with high-end bath and bed linens.

She carried the oil lamp back into the kitchen and set it down on the counter beside the first-aid kit. "So do you not have electricity at all, or is this a temporary power outage?"

"I haven't tried the lights. It's usually pretty reliable, though."

"Then why in the world am I trying to patch you up in the dark?"

"I prefer to live simply."

Simply? The very word made her shudder. Give her every electrical convenience modern technology could summon up, thank you very much. She liked her zoned air-conditioning, and her blow dryer, and towel warmer and wireless-Internet-capable cell phone/camera/television.

"Oh, for heaven's sake. Where's a light switch? I need to see what I'm doing."

He sighed and pressed a rocker switch on the wall beside him. Bright halogen lights imbedded in the beams overhead suddenly shone down, making her squint for several moments. Tom's wound came into focus.

"This definitely needs stitches. It's pretty deep."

"Just slap some butterflies on it and call it good," he growled.

She sighed. "All right, but you're going to have to be careful. I don't know if butterflies will hold or not."

He threw her a look so hot it made her bare toes bend into hard little knots of anticipation. "I can be careful," he murmured. "Very careful."

Her hands inexplicably shaky, she tore open a half-dozen sterile wrappings and laid the butterflies out on the counter as he turned his back to her.

"Are you always this cussedly independent?" she asked as she gently drew the edges of the wound together and commenced taping them in place.

"Nope. I'm usually worse."

"Great." She finished with the butterflies and laid a strip of rayon over the wound, covered it with gauze pads and secured it all with long strips of adhesive tape. She studied the bandage, pondering its chances of staying in place. Not good. She rummaged in the first-aid kit and found an elastic bandage. Perfect.

She held one end of the long, beige wrap against his left side and passed the three-inch-wide strip under his right arm. Her palms skimmed across his ribs, and her own stomach couldn't help but contract at the way the slabbed muscles of his abdomen tensed into impressive ridges under her touch. To reach all the way around him to pass the bandage from her right hand to her left, she had to lay her cheek against his chest and all but hug him. His big body radiated enough heat to scald her.

Her hands wanted to stray lower, to test his desire for her. Sheesh! The poor guy was hurt, for goodness' sake, and here she was, pawing him like some sex-starved desperado. Except, at the moment, she felt *exactly* like a sex-starved desperado.

She jerked back, startled by the thought. She did *not* chase after guys. She didn't even particularly crave sex! Yet here she was, her palms itching to run all over his naked body. Must be some weird hormonal reaction to almost dying.

Forcing herself to pay attention to the job at hand, she moved around behind him, passing the bandage carefully across the cut and leaning forward to reach around him again, this time from the back. And again, a visceral need, electric and disturbing, ripped through her as she hugged his athletic form. Wouldn't you know it—the end of the bandage ran out smack dab on top of his stomach. She ducked under his raised arm to pin the end of the bandage in place.

And made the mistake of looking up at him. His eyes blazed, black as night, consumed by a fire that incinerated her to her very fingertips. *Yowza.* She jerked her hands away from him, and actually glanced down at her palms to see if the skin burned from touching him. Her every nerve felt raw and exposed.

She stumbled backward, staring at his back hungrily as he carried the first-aid kit into the bathroom. She looked away hastily as he came out. He offered her the bathroom for a solo shower and she didn't hesitate to take him up on the offer. Did cold showers work on women, too?

She chickened out on testing the theory and opted instead for the relaxation of a nice, hot shower. However, when she finally turned the water off and stepped out into the bathroom, she was appalled to see a neatly folded man's T-shirt lying on the counter beside the sink.

He'd come into the bathroom while she was bathing? Her gaze whipped around to the shower door, and she was relieved—and disappointed—to see it was milky glass with wavy patterns through it.

"Hungry?" he asked as she slid onto one of the bar stools.

"I don't know. I suppose so." She'd been so wrapped up in staying alive and then her inexplicable reaction to him that she hadn't stopped to think about anything as mundane as food. But now that he mentioned it, she realized she was ravenous. And *thirsty.*

He set a beautiful double old-fashioned glass on the counter in front of her. The elegantly carved crystal caught the light from overhead and cast prisms all over the mahogany kitchen cabinets. She recognized the crystal pattern. Her brows lifted slightly. Waterford crystal? Who *was* this solitary pilot for hire? Silently, he poured water from a pitcher he took from the brushed stainless-steel refrigerator for her. She drank down the whole glass in a few gulps. He filled it again, seeming to know that she'd be desperately thirsty.

He went to the refrigerator and emerged with a green and yellow fruit about the size of his fist. He pulled a knife out of a drawer and peeled and sliced it efficiently. He stabbed a piece of the fruit and held it out to her on the end of the knife.

"Mango," he announced.

She nodded and took the juicy fruit. It was sweet, a cross between a peach and an orange. Odd, but tasty.

"Are you sure this place belongs to you?" she asked dubiously.

He frowned at her. "Yeah. Why?"

"It doesn't seem to…fit you."

He glanced around. "What's wrong with it? You don't like my decorating taste?"

He'd decorated this place? "Nothing's wrong with it." That was the point. It was too perfect. Too elegant, too…classy. This was the sort of place she'd pick for herself. But he…he was rough around the edges. Primal. She'd picture him in a beach shack with empty beer bottles and old pizza boxes overflowing the trash can. She opened her mouth. Closed it again.

He glanced at her wryly as if he knew what she was thinking. He turned away and fiddled with putting his water glass in the sink. "You can sleep on the couch."

"Where are you sleeping?" she blurted.

He cocked an eyebrow at her. "Why? Are you offering to share my bed?"

Just how tempted she was at the idea shocked her into silence. It was all well and good to be turned on by this guy but to sleep with him? That was a big step.

To get naked with him…to experience all that masculine power unleashed…to completely let go of her inhibitions with him…

Man, it was tempting. And totally out of character for her. Obviously, she was suffering some sort of strange aftereffect of the accident and her brush with death. She'd regret it tomorrow if she took him up on his offer tonight. Reluctantly, she shook her head. "Thanks for the offer, but I'd better not."

He frowned, almost as if confused. Opened his mouth to say something, but then closed it again. He turned off the overhead lights and left the room without speaking. At least he left her the oil lamp. In its soft glow, she turned to face the couch, which was underneath a wide picture window that framed a magnificent view of the ocean below. Even in the darkness, she could make out the rolling and crashing white of the breakers rushing in toward the beach. Drawn to the view, she moved over to the window. A light rain whipped around the *bure,* driven by a sharp breeze. Cyclone Kato was beginning to breathe upon them.

She started when something heavy thunked down behind her. Jumpy, she whipped her head around. Tom had just dropped a blanket, pillow and sheets on the coffee table.

He shrugged apologetically. "I'd sleep on the couch, but it's too short for me, and with my back, I'll need to lie on my stomach."

She smiled understandingly at him, grateful that he was being a gentleman about the sleeping arrangement. Truth be told, she felt like a heel for climbing all over him, but then turning him down when he took her up on her unspoken offer. "I don't mind sleeping out here. The couch will fit me just fine."

He nodded once, turned and disappeared on silent, bare feet into the bedroom. Suddenly, she was so exhausted she could hardly see straight. Mechanically, she made up the couch into a bed. She left the oil lamp burning. For some reason, she wasn't quite ready to face the dark and her suddenly overactive imagination. She stretched out on the couch.

As exhausted as she was, her brain wouldn't unwind enough for her to immediately contemplate going to sleep. She lay there for a long time. Eventually, she forced herself to extinguish the lamp and still, sleep eluded her.

Without warning, it all hit her. The terrifying plane crash, the desperate swim for her life, the shock of finding out about the attack on the beach. She started to shiver, and then to shake. And then the tears came. At first they were no more than hot streaks down her cheeks, but before long they'd blossomed into racking sobs. She turned her face into the pillow to muffle the sound, but for the life of her she couldn't stop the sobs from coming.

She started violently when a male voice rumbled from above her, "Oh, for crying out loud."

Reluctantly, she looked up at his dark form within the larger darkness of the room. Even as exasperated as he sounded, his presence was insanely comforting.

He rumbled, "I suppose you want me to hug you and tell you everything will be all right, don't you?"

Miffed at the humor lacing his voice, she snapped, "Far be it from me to force you into such an onerous task."

He made a noise that could have been laughter bitten off sharply. But she wasn't sure. He sighed and sat down on the couch beside her. "Fine. Come here."

She sniffed, "No, that's all right."

He ignored her and gathered her up in his arms, drawing her easily into his lap, surrounding her in his big, comfortable embrace. As hard as she tried to stop it, the floodgates opened up again. She sobbed into his shoulder for several minutes before it dawned on her that his shoulder was naked. And warm. And sexy.

And in an instant, the nature of their hug changed completely. She felt it in the way his arms suddenly tightened around her, in the electric energy zinging between them, in the sudden pounding of his heart underneath her ear. Despite herself, her own pulse accelerated, her breathing growing shallow and fast. She was *not* going to randomly crawl all over him, darn it! Her lust for him was just a reaction to her near death experience. Nothing more. She wasn't actually attracted to him in the least.

Liar.

When his finger tipped her chin up to him, she didn't fight it. When she gazed up into the dark planes and shadows of his face, she didn't say anything to forestall what was coming. And when his head started down toward hers, her lips parted in breathless anticipation. Nope, not attracted to him in the least.

Chapter 3

Tom inhaled the scent of her, female and faintly sweet beneath an overlay of deodorant soap, unable to stop himself from wanting to inhale the rest of her. Sex poured off her in powerful waves that belied her feeble attempt at maintaining her distance from him.

When her sobs first woke him, he'd been asleep in his bed, dreaming disturbing images of fire and water and spiderwebs. He'd have to talk to Joe, the local bartender, about the quality of the whiskey the guy was stocking these days. He really wished he could remember how he'd ended up on that beach with that woman draped all over him.

Maybe Joe could shed some light on that, too. When he didn't just stay home and drink himself into a stupor alone, the other place he went to drown his sorrows was Joe's place, the Paradise Lost Bar & Grill. That would undoubtedly be where he'd picked up Maddie.

Her name rocketed through him. As clear as a bell, the moment came back to him, a bolt out of the blue. He'd stared, shocked, into her light green eyes as she introduced herself. None of the context of the moment came with the memory, though. Not the setting nor any conversation before or after. Just that one disembodied moment. "Hi. I'm Madeline-and-I-prefer-not-to-be-called-Maddie."

She'd looked just like Arielle. *Just* like Arielle. The same willfulness gleamed in her striking green eyes, the same determination was apparent in her firm handshake. They were two women who knew what they wanted and both went after it full bore.

Maybe Arielle was a little more exotic in her features. But Maddie—how could he *not* call her that after she'd made such a point of it? He loved the fire in her eyes when she got hot and bothered—definitely looked less dissipated. Arielle had been an exceptionally hard-partying girl, and at age twenty-four, her lifestyle was beginning to take its toll on her looks. Although he'd place Maddie in her mid-to-late-twenties, she seemed worlds more...grown up. Heh. Not hard to achieve in comparison to Arielle, who had been a pampered and extremely spoiled pop star since her early teens.

Maddie snuggled closer as if she was cold, and he pulled the blanket across both of them. Nope, definitely not Madeline material. Maddie just seemed to fit her better.

Why had an obviously classy lady like her condescended to spend time with a guy like him, anyway? What did she want from him? Unfortunately, suspicion of everyone and everything came with his line of work. Well, his former line of work. He used to be a bodyguard. A damned good one. Fought over by a who's who of international celebrities. Until Arielle. Or rather, until she died. On his watch.

Damn, he needed a drink.

He'd noticed several new bottles of whiskey in the cabinet in his room earlier. He shook off the memory of Arielle's dead, green eyes staring up vacantly, her back arched in death spasms, her blond hair matted black with dried blood. He swore silently to himself. How rude would it be to dump Maddie off his lap and make a beeline for the liquor cabinet?

Probably unforgivably rude. And he really liked the warm, soft, cuddly feel of her in his lap like this. She fit just right against his chest, her forehead tucked against his neck, her arms wrapped lightly around his ribs. Holding her, like he was now, was…comforting. Made him feel not so alone. He wasn't lonely, of course, he told himself hastily. But a hug felt nice now and again. Even to a bastard like him.

Maddie's sobs renewed themselves, although quieter this time. She swiped at her eyes, dashing away tears, then tucked her fist under her chin, childlike. He recognized the body language. She was crying out some sort of trauma that had transformed itself into a desperate need for comfort. Any kind of comfort. A cuddle, or sex or whatever. And he happened to be the nearest able-bodied male able to fill her need. And Lord knew, he was willing.

No guy in his right mind would care about being used for comfort sex by a woman this hot. Not that he'd been in his right mind for the past six months or so. But still. He was totally okay with being this woman's shoulder sponge and sex toy.

Alarm jolted him. Jeez. What if *he* was the cause of her being this upset? He racked his brain. What boneheaded thing had he said or done to her within the massive black gap yawning tauntingly in his memory?

He worked through the logic quickly. She wouldn't have come home with him if he'd hurt her or been rude to her, would she? Was she on the rebound from some other jerk, maybe?

He swore under his breath. He really had to cut back on the booze. He couldn't recall a damned thing about the past day or so.

Thing was, Tom sighed, he knew better than to be some socialite's casual beach fling like this. He'd watched Arielle blast through men like a demolition derby driver, leaving a messy trail of wrecked lives in her wake. The sour taste of it in his mouth washed away the lingering traces of Maddie's impossibly sexy scent.

He probably ought to do something to draw her out of her crying jag. She'd been at it for a while now. He sighed. Ever the good guy, he was. It was probably why he never got the girl. He'd vowed to hang up his good guy white hat once and for all when he came here to the end of the world. But apparently, a few vestiges of it lingered, dammit.

Instead of kissing her like he'd originally intended, he halted, his mouth inches from hers. "Can you feel it?" he murmured.

"Feel what?"

"Blood flowing through your veins. Air moving in and out of your lungs. Heat on your skin."

She blinked a couple of times as if she was having trouble registering the meaning of his words. Lost in a sexual haze, was she? An instant of male triumph surged in his gut. So, sue him. Yeah, he got a rush out of turning on a good-looking woman.

He half whispered, "We made it to shelter before the storm. We're safe. Doesn't it feel great just to be alive?"

Her eyes were big and wide as she gazed up at him in the dim lamplight. Sudden, intense awareness of their bodies rushed over her face as plain as day. He didn't have to see her blush to feel its sudden heat radiating off her. She swayed closer to him, her fingers toying with his chest hair in unconscious flirtation.

He could *so* have her right now. And she'd *so* hate him for it in the morning. He sighed and drew back slightly. He wasn't the kind of jerk who took advantage of a woman when her emotional defenses were down. He might want to be that kind of unfeeling ass, but it just wasn't in him to take advantage of any female like that. Not to mention he had no intention of dragging anyone else into the train wreck of his life. Despite the occasional one-night stand, at the end of the day he wanted to be alone. End of discussion.

Except, a small voice whispered at the back of his head, *Maddie feels damned good in your arms.*

He ought to invite her into his bed, not for wild bunny sex, but just to hold her and make her feel safe so she could sleep. But panic flitted through him at the idea. No one was allowed into his bedroom. Ever. It was his last retreat, his most private, personal sanctuary.

Instead he offered, "Do you want me to sit with you until you fall asleep?"

One perfectly plucked eyebrow curved up at him. "Do I look like a five-year-old?"

He tilted his head and studied her. "Nah. I'd put you at nine or ten at least."

Her mouth pursed in disapproval, but her anxious eyes told a different tale altogether. And he noticed she wasn't making any aggressive move to remove herself from the circle of his arms.

He let her off the hook and announced in a tone that brooked no argument, "You're lying back down here on the couch, and I'm moving over to that armchair and not budging until I hear you snoring."

She laughed. "I don't snore!"

"I bet you do."

"Do not," she retorted indignantly.

He grinned down at her. *Better.* "I'll let you know." He let go of her and went to stand. But he hadn't counted on the lady having other ideas.

"Don't move," she whispered, looping her arms around his neck.

"But—"

She cut him off. "I want to listen to your heart beat. It lets me know you're really alive. When I was swimming to shore—I didn't know if we would live or die—I was so scared—and it was so dark…"

She'd had some sort of drowning scare? When was that? She was talking as if he already knew about it. Dammit. She'd no doubt confessed all the gory details while he was drunk off his ass. Unfortunately, he wasn't one of those men who got loud and obnoxious when he was wasted. People often mistook him for being much more sober than he was.

Maybe her big scare was how he'd gotten her into the sack with him in the first place. He'd played the "I can keep you safe, little lady" card. And at one point, that might have been true. Before Arielle got killed—stabbed to death by a stalker fan—when he'd been in charge of her security detail.

Careful not to promise to protect her, he thought and gathered Maddie close. "You're safe now. Everything's fine."

Except apparently, everything was not fine. She wriggled in his arms until he turned her loose. He expected her to climb out of his lap, but noooo…she threw her left leg across his hips and straddled him. Right there on the couch. Groin to groin. Pressing down on him just like she would if they were making love. Only a few pieces of flimsy cloth kept him from plunging up into her wet, tight heat, of sliding her up and down his length until he forgot everything and exploded…

Jeez! What the hell was wrong with him tonight?

She laid her right ear against his heart and stilled, listening intently. And for some reason, it was one of the sexiest things a woman had ever done to him. Maybe because it was real. A reaching out for human connection at the most fundamental level of existence. Confirmation of a simple heartbeat. And it all but pushed him over the edge.

"We're alive," she murmured in awe. "Both of us."

Ohh-kay. Poor kid had definitely had some sort of major fright recently. "Uh, yeah," he mumbled. "Alive. Miraculous, isn't it?" More like a nightmare from where he sat, but he wasn't going to quibble with her about the relative benefits of being alive or dead while she was straddling him like a cowgirl about to ride him until his knees buckled.

"It's a wild thing inside me, this feeling of having cheated death."

Oh, Lord. He knew exactly the sensation she was talking about. It tore through a person like chain lightning, making every inch a soul tingle, every nerve jangle on edge, every breath a triumph. Blood pounded through him, hot and thick, and abruptly he could count his pulse in the throbbing of his male flesh, so hard and needy he couldn't stand it.

Gritting his teeth against an urge to throw her down and drive himself into her until they both screamed, he managed to force out, "Honey, you're going to have to climb off me or be prepared to do something about where you're sitting because I'm about to have some serious self-control issues."

She laughed. She *laughed!*

A noise escaped the back of his throat. Whether a growl

or a groan, he couldn't exactly say. But it made her jerk her head up off his chest and stare at him, startled, her eyes big and wide and...have mercy...*aware*.

He actually saw her breath hitch. Her chest started to lift, then hesitated, then finished the breath. He closed his eyes in pain. Must. Not. Do. This.

She made a little sound, a soft, "Oh," that shot through him like a fifty-thousand-volt taser. And then she leaned forward as if to kiss him. Except the movement also had the effect of rocking her gently against parts of him that didn't need any more rocking at the moment. She froze, her pupils black in the subtle, and suddenly unbearably sensual, light suffusing the room.

He muttered, "Yeah. That."

She melted on top of him, flowing over him like warm honey, her body softening and relaxing against his. Her hands slid over his shoulders to toy with the short hairs at the back of his neck. Her breasts came to rest against him, hard nipples cushioned in the gently resilient softness of her breasts. Her thighs opened wider, pressing her even more firmly against him.

He closed his eyes. Threw his head back against the sofa cushions in an agony of need so great he barely noticed his back protesting. And damned if she didn't lick his throat. She really had to quit that licking bit unless she planned to lick all of him. Soon. Hands tugged at his head, drawing it forward once more. And then she was kissing him, her mouth open and wet and inviting. How could a guy say no to being eaten alive like this?

His own adrenaline rush answered hers. He had no idea where it came from, but it tore through him like a tornado. With her body surfing his, sliding across him with her mouth—with her whole self—he rose up to meet her helplessly.

Her hands fumbled at his waist, untying the drawstring of his shorts. She lifted up enough to slide them down his hips, and then he was spilling into her hands, hard and hot and jumping beneath her touch.

"Oh, my," she sighed.

She had to quit that sighing thing, too. It was driving him out of his mind. He reached forward, lifting the hem of her— his—shirt off her. She rose out of his lap, a naked nymph called forth from the heart of nature, perfect. Ethereal. Beautiful. Her breasts were high and firm, not large, but beautifully shaped. With a chest like that, she ought to walk around topless all the time. He restrained the urge to reach for the pale mounds and just looked at them, savoring the way they rose and fell with her rapid, shallow breathing. His gaze traced the slim inward curve of her waist, the gentle flare of her hips, the shadowed place where their bodies met.

"Well, touch me, already!" she demanded.

He glanced up at her, startled. And grinned. "Sorry. I was enjoying the view."

She leaned down and kissed him voraciously, biting his lower lip hard enough to draw his undivided attention to her mouth. *Vixen.* He slid a hand up to the back of her head under her silky hair, anchoring her in place as he took control of the kiss, plunging his tongue inside her mouth. It tasted of the ocean, salty and primeval. It called him home. He sucked at her, drinking in her sighs, devouring the taste of her, the smooth slide of her tongue against his, the way she surged against him.

He skimmed his fingertips down her body, and she stretched sinuously under the light caress, inflaming the inferno already raging inside him. "Yup, you're definitely alive," he murmured.

She arched her back, rocking her hips against his provocatively. Except now there was nothing between them, just hot, slick flesh on hot, slick flesh.

He leaned forward, wrapped his arms around her and lifted her up and away from him. "Are you sure about this?" he murmured.

"I'm not sure about anything except that by some miracle we made it. We're here. We're *alive.*"

He could wait no longer. He plunged into all that vibrant exuberance and groaned when she cried out in joy. His buttocks clenched until they nearly cramped, driving him up and into all that heat and energy, hot and tight upon him and around him. He touched her very core, and it pulsed against him once. Twice. He surged beneath her, drawn into her as if she was a force of nature. Her internal muscles milked him powerfully, sucking life from the very dregs of his soul. And he gave it all to her. He pumped into her with abandon, holding her hips down to push into her more and more deeply.

The sea roared outside and he shouted his release inside. She threw her head back and let out a keening, shuddering cry of pleasure that broke something loose within his soul. Something he'd not even known was bottled up within him. He collapsed as new awareness of it, of her, of himself, flooded over him.

Wonder suffused his consciousness. Indeed, she was right about one thing. He was *alive.* For the first time in a long time. Since before Arielle. Before…

Inexplicably, the end of the thought slipped away from him. Before what? How long had it been since he'd felt like this? His short-term memory might be shot to hell, but his long-term memory was just fine, thank you very much. And he couldn't remember the last time he'd felt this good.

"Mmm." She curled up in his arms, his wild, elemental force of nature back to being a kitten once more, limp and sleepy.

"You need to rest," he murmured.

"You, too," she murmured back drowsily. "Big night. Almost dying and all."

He had no idea what she was talking about. The cut on his back? It was no big deal. Annoying, yes. But life-threatening? No. The only threat some guy with a knife posed to them was catching him drunk enough not to defend them. The bastard had come close to that tonight. But it wouldn't happen again, Tom vowed silently to himself. As long as Maddie was with him, he would not get so drunk that he blacked out or that he couldn't fend off some asshole with a blade.

Tightening his arms around her, he leaned forward. She made a sound of protest as he stood up with her in his arms, but she settled quickly against his chest. He laid her down gently on the couch, tucking the blankets in around her chin.

"Sleep," he murmured, smoothing her hair away from her creamy brow. There was something eminently satisfying about making love to a woman until she lost consciousness. He watched her eyelashes flutter down. She was out like a light in a matter of seconds.

His arms felt unaccountably empty and he frowned at the sensation. True to his word though, he sat down gingerly in the armchair opposite her. After their athletics, his back stung like hell. But it was worth it. And how.

He propped his feet up on the end table he'd carved last month in a failed attempt to climb out of the bottle. His sharp eyes picked out her profile against the larger blackness of the storm outside. The seas were worse than he'd ever seen them. Vague memory of a storm approaching tickled his consciousness.

He and Maddie had stirred up quite a storm of their own in here, tonight. Fascinating woman. A study in contrasts. Calculating the odds of turning their now two-night stand into a three-peat, he locked his fingers across his stomach and settled in to watch over her.

An uncomfortable sensation of déjà vu crept over him. He used to watch over Arielle like this wherever she happened to pass out after one of her wild escapades. She used to tell him to quit hovering over her like a nervous mother hen, to go get some sleep in a real bed. She actually thought she could out-stubborn him. It had never worked. But she'd never given up trying.

Right up till that last night. He'd been ready to strangle her for insisting on going out on an evening when he was not only off duty but had other plans. But he'd never broken the implacable calm that was part and parcel of his job. Bodyguards weren't supposed to show emotion, and they certainly weren't supposed to throttle their impulsive, immature, spoiled, self-destructive clients. Even if the client richly deserved it. Not even if the client snuck out when her chief of security was out and her other guards were sleeping, and the client went and got themselves carved up by a nutcase. But it didn't stop him from wanting to wrap his hands around Arielle's neck and squeeze some sense into her.

Nor were bodyguards supposed to seduce females in their living rooms and make love to them until they screamed, even if *they* richly deserved it, too. Particularly when the poor woman was clearly upset and exhausted. What Maddie had needed was a decent night's sleep.

But in spite of what he should have done, he couldn't stop relishing what had happened. Images of Maddie in the throes of screaming pleasure danced across his mind. As he sat there in the dark, listening to her quiet breathing, fantasies of her crawling all over his willing body again and again in as many different ways as his imagination could conjure stole his breath away. Who'd have guessed he had such a vivid imagination?

Desperate to distract himself, he listened to the storm gathering steam outside. *Kato*. The name popped into his head. A moment later, its meaning came back to him as well. That was the name of the cyclone spinning in toward Vanua Taru. He hated it how these random snippets of memory kept dropping into his mind like capricious gifts from a prankster deity.

The ocean sounded furious below. Like a woman whose lover, almost in her grasp, had been stolen out from under her nose. What an odd thought that was. But then, this had been an odd night all around.

If these rain bands got much worse, the island would be completely shut down by morning, cyclone or no. That could be a problem since he had food and drink in the house for one. He hadn't expected to ride out the cyclone with company. He had some shopping to do, assuming he could convince her to stay with him until Kato passed. Three or four days marooned in his villa with nothing to do but listen to the storm and try out a couple dozen of his fantasies sounded like a little slice of paradise.

Looked like a trip to town was in order first thing tomorrow—or rather, later today. Given the searing pain in his back, he'd probably have to give in and get some stitches in his back, too. Which would also give him a chance to tell the sheriff about the attack on the beach.

He frowned, considering the chances of the attacker escaping the island before Kato hit. He bloody well wouldn't fly in this weather, and neither would any of the other island-taxi pilots. People wishing to leave Vanua Taru would be down to ferry service or private boats. Joe the bartender, also the local ferry pilot, was extremely stingy about sailing his precious ferryboat in heavy seas. The Merry Widow was probably already tucked safely in her boathouse and not likely to emerge until after the storm. Unless the attacker had his own boat and a death wish, he wasn't going anywhere until Kato passed. Nope, the Sex on the Beach Killer was stuck on Vanua Taru for at least the next several days. If that was, in fact, who'd attacked them.

Without any great heat, the thought that he could use a drink passed through his mind. But it was overridden by a much more pressing concern. He seriously didn't need to be trapped on this tiny piece of real estate with some crazy bastard looking to slice folks into bits. Truth be told, the thought made his blood run cold. Six months ago, he'd have laughed at the prospect. Back then he was still invincible. Had still never lost a client. He'd still been the baddest badass bodyguard in the biz. Nothing had gotten past him. But all that had been before.

And besides, Maddie was with him now. He had her safety to think about.

A flash of Arielle's bloody corpse flashed through his mind's eye. By some trick of his imagination, or maybe his subconscious, the face in his memory morphed from Arielle's into Maddie's. And suddenly he felt sick to his stomach.

Shaken to his core, he unfolded quietly from the chair and made his unsteady way into his bedroom. *Go away!* he screamed at the image of Maddie's dead face stuck in his mind. Oh, God. Please go away. No. No. Not another one dead on his watch.

His hands shaking so badly he could hardly hold the door knob, he managed to lock the door. Clumsily, he tested the knob to be sure it was secure. Safely barricaded in his private hell, he headed for the tall cabinet in the corner. Gut churning, he opened the door and stared at his wide selection of poisons. Tonight, he needed something fast and brutal—180 proof grain alcohol. Guaranteed to wipe the brain clean of unbearable memories in ten minutes flat.

Come to papa.

Too rattled to bother with a glass—not that he usually bothered with one anymore—he picked up the bottle. A pair of green, laughing eyes swam before him. The flash of a knife. Green eyes wide with fear. He lowered the bottle without taking a drink. Turned to head for his bathroom. *Green eyes, shining with pleasure after mind-blowing sex.*

He tipped the bottle…and poured the contents down the sink. The amber liquid swirled into oblivion just as green eyes swirled around him. Madeline's eyes…Arielle's eyes… accusing eyes he'd failed to protect…a green-eyed girl who'd died because of him…would die again…

Chapter 4

Maddie blinked awake in a gray gloom that was half morning and half something else indeterminate. Rain lashed against the window above her head, and she lay there, listening to it groggily while she assessed the pain shooting through her literally from her head to her feet. It was the sharp discomfort of overexertion so violent as to be abuse to her body. Not since she'd reinvented herself from curvaceous farm girl to rail-thin high-society girl had she hurt like this.

How in the world had she gotten so sore—

Oh. Yeah.

The plane crash. The swim for her life. Dragging Tom ashore.

Of course that didn't account for all her aches and pains. A few of them in places that had nothing to do with swimming and everything to do with throwing herself wildly at a complete stranger and humping his brains out. Heat sprang to her cheeks as memory of her wanton assault on her host last night came back to her.

What in the world had gotten into her? She didn't do things like that. Ever. Heck, she didn't even particularly *like* sex. Not even after a few too many drinks. Of course, she didn't much like alcohol, either. But she'd been worse than drunk last night. She'd been…horny. It was a complete anomaly for her. No doubt some sort of survival reflex. Nothing more than that. She'd been overwrought. Burning off adrenaline. Blown away to be alive. She probably ought to be grateful the guy didn't look and smell like a troll. As it was, her morning-after regrets weren't so bad. The guy was a hunk, after all. Even if he was basically a beach bum. Really. It was nothing personal between her and Tom.

Yeah. That was it. Nothing personal. He would understand that. Heck, he'd been as edgy as she'd been, as revved up on an adrenaline surge of his own. Survival sex. That was all it had been.

Of course, she had no idea if such a thing actually even existed. It sounded good, though. Besides, if it didn't exist, it should. She groaned and rolled carefully onto her back, daggers of pain shooting through her. She was one giant cramp from head to toe. She subsided on the sofa cushions. Whatever kind of sex they'd engaged in last night, she had to admit, it had been unbelievably good.

She lifted her arm just enough to see her watch, which was probably toast after last night's wild events. Wow. It still appeared to be working. Gotta love those Swiss watchmakers. Hers was apparently going strong after surviving an explosion and spending hours dunked in salt water. Then the actual time caught her attention. Almost noon? Her jaw dropped. She rarely slept past seven o'clock and *never* past nine. A lifetime of getting up to do her morning farm chores at five o'clock had seen to that.

Using the back of the sofa to lever herself upright by slow, painful degrees, she eventually managed to look out the window at the ocean below. The raging surf had all but swallowed the beach. Only a narrow strip of sand was left and the largest of the waves rolled into the base of the rocks below, sending up plumes of spray. The water was a dull, metallic gray, partially obscured by the lighter gray curtain of rain, blowing across it in sheets. So much for Paradise Cove, the sunny island resort she'd come to evaluate for her travel agency employer.

She glanced around the spacious room. Where was Tom? No sign of him yet. Of course, his night had been every bit as rough as hers had been. She climbed to her feet, her joints all but creaking aloud, and shuffled to the bathroom like an arthritic patient.

At least her underwear, which she'd washed and rinsed out last night, was dry this morning. It wasn't much, but it was one small, intact piece of her from before the plane crash. She shimmied into the lacy black-satin bra and panty set and felt worlds better.

Then she spied herself in the mirror. And stared, appalled. No makeup, no hairdo and nothing but a baggy T-shirt swathing her in what seemed like acres of olive-green cotton. If anyone she knew in Chicago saw her now, they wouldn't recognize her! Madeline C. had been taken over by a disheveled stranger. At least, a stranger to them…she recognized the alien, and it made her shudder. Maddie Crummby was back.

Panic clawed the inside of her rib cage, seeking release. No! Not after all her hard work! Two painstaking years of creating an image, building a new persona of herself from the ground up…she wouldn't let a single, disastrous night ruin it all!

Using the lone pocket comb sitting on the bathroom counter, she painstakingly put her hair back into order. Thank God she had a great cut. Even unstyled and left to air-dry, or pillow-dry as the case might be, it fell in bouncy layers around her shoulders.

If only she had some makeup. She felt positively naked like this. Not only her regular kit, but also her emergency back-up bag of makeup, were at the bottom of the South Pacific. Some lucky mermaid was going to have a great time with her top-of-the-line designer collection of cosmetics. Maddie hated to think what it was going to cost to replace all of it.

Frantic for something, anything, that might work to restore Madeline C. to the mirror in front of her, she hunted through Tom's drawers. She pounced with a cry of joy when she spotted a probable-looking tube wedged in the back of one of the drawers. Some former "guest" must have left the mascara here. Bless her, whoever she was. More searching in the dark recesses at the back of the drawer yielded a little pot of maroon lip gloss even a hooker would think twice about wearing.

The cosmetics were drugstore brands Madeline C. would never *dream* of using except in this, the direst of emergencies. But sometimes a girl just couldn't be picky. She opened the mascara tube and pulled out the applicator brush. Dried out and gloppy. Hyperventilation threatened. She could handle this. She could make it work. Think, *think!* What would a chic, in-charge sort of woman do now?

She rummaged again, this time through Tom's medicine cabinet, which she dimly noted in the midst of her panic was an orderly affair sporting some rather snazzy brands of men's grooming products.

Aha! Baby oil. Perfect. She added a dab of it to the tube and worked it in vigorously with the applicator until it regained a credible consistency. She brushed some on her lashes. She went easy with it because it turned out to be a true-black mascara instead of the more understated black-brown she preferred. But it would do. A tiny dab of the lurid maroon lip gloss diluted in the palm of her hand with some talcum powder and she had a crude, pale pink blush. She massaged it into her cheeks carefully. Wouldn't want to look like a clown, now would she? She shuddered to recall her first efforts at makeup application after her move to Chicago.

A tiny bit of the full-strength gloss on her lips—just enough to give them a little extra color—and she was starting to look halfway presentable again. She surveyed her emergency makeover critically in the mirror. Blotted off a little of the gloss. There. Better. Not half bad, given what she had to work with. Visceral relief flowed through her gut at having her Madeline C. armor back in place. Odd. She never used to wear makeup at all. Ahh, if she'd only known in high school what she knew now about grooming and self-presentation. She'd have knocked the boys dead and made cheerleader for sure.

Not that she'd regretted going through high school largely invisible. That, too, had had its advantages. Still, it was strange how dependent she'd apparently become on her makeup. Equally strange was her desperate need for some of it before she faced Tom Laruso this morning after…well, after.

Was her transformation all part and parcel of some deep-seated identity crisis or something? She frowned, considering it, until she remembered that frowning prematurely aged a person's facial skin and caused wrinkles. She carefully went through the breathing exercises to relax and smooth out all of her facial muscles. Supposedly, if she mastered keeping her face perfectly relaxed all the time, she would never need Botox to stave off wrinkles.

She opened her eyes once more. Nah, this was nothing as deeply psychological as an identity crisis. She simply wanted to catch a good man and marry well. There was nothing wrong with taking good care of herself. Okay, obsessively perfect care of herself. Maybe she was a teensy bit whacked. She'd calm down after she had a three-carat diamond on her finger and the I dos had been traded.

She could really use some of her own clothes. This hideous T-shirt was barely better than a burlap sack by way of style and appeal. She spied a leather belt hanging on a hook on the back of the bathroom door and appropriated it. Cinched in around her waist and carefully folded into wide pleats, the T-shirt didn't make a half-bad minidress. Thankfully, she'd just had her legs waxed, and the past two weeks spent evaluating other swanky Fijian resorts had given her a great tan. She looked pretty good in the shirt now, if she said so herself.

And with that thought, Madeline C. was finally back in charge. Calmer, cooler and already feeling worlds more sophisticated.

Thus restored, she stepped out of the bathroom. Still no sign of Tom. She puttered around the main room for nearly an hour, and even read a months-old woodworking magazine out of sheer desperation. How did he survive with no TV, no Internet, heck, not even a radio that she could find?

Finally, in grave danger of losing her marbles completely from boredom, she moved over to his bedroom door and stared at it. Should she wake him up? He really ought to be up by now. Maybe he had some sort of concussion and was in trouble. After all, he'd been unconscious a long time after the crash. Yup, she'd better wake him up.

Her boredom thus armed with a semblance of logic, she knocked on the door, butterflies jumping in her stomach. No answer. She knocked harder. Still no answer. Alarm blossomed for real in her throat. Had something happened to him? She reached for the doorknob, hesitated and then turned it. Or tried to. It was locked.

Oh, God. What if he'd gone into shock in there? Slipped into a coma? Died?

"Tom!" she called. "Wake up!" Slapping her palms painfully against the heavy wood panel, she pounded frantically on the door.

It flew open beneath her fists and he burst out into the main room. His hair stood up in every direction and his shorts and T-shirt were rumpled. But his eyes were fully alert, roving the room quickly. Danger poured off him, and—*good Lord, that was a gun in his right fist.*

"What's wrong?" he bit out. Death vibrated in his voice. He hooked her with his left arm, pulling her behind him as he scanned the *bure,* ready and obviously willing to kill. He all but shoved her through the doorway into his bedroom.

"Uh, nothing's wrong, Tom. I was just worried about you. You were sleeping so late and I thought you might have a concussion or something…"

Tom's tall frame sagged. He turned slowly. Glared at her blearily. "Good God, woman, you'd wake the dead with the racket you're making. Pipe down before you rupture my skull with that shrieking."

"I'm not shrieking," she retorted indignantly.

His gaze narrowed into a distinctly menacing expression. "You're still shrieking."

She frowned. "Headache?"

"Splitting."

She recalled seeing a bottle of aspirin in the bathroom. She stepped around him gingerly, made her way as quietly as she could to the medicine cabinet and pulled out four pills. After all, he looked as if he had the mother of all headaches. When she stepped back out into the main room, he was seated at the breakfast bar, his elbows propped on the granite surface and his head cradled in his hands. She poured him a big glass of water and set the pills in front of him.

"Can I make you breakfast?" she offered.

He scowled at her over the rim of the glass. Not in the mood for food, then. Well, she was hungry. She opened the refrigerator. Typical bachelor stash. A few beers, some steak sauce and a crusty bottle of mustard. A jar of olives, a few other random condiments and a couple of pieces of local fruit. She did find a half-dozen eggs, some bacon and a can of Cheez Whiz, though. Mmm. Tasty. Hardening-of-the-arteries in a can. The freezer yielded a loaf of bread, but that was about it for useful food.

"I thought there was a hurricane coming this way," she remarked as she laid the frozen bread on a cookie sheet to broil in the oven for toast and pulled out a skillet to fry the bacon.

"There is."

"You don't have a whole lot of supplies laid in that I can see. Shouldn't you have a week or two supply of food and drinking water? Some candles or something?"

"I've got everything stored elsewhere. The power will go out and refrigerated food will spoil."

Ah. That made sense. Still, he should eat. In her limited experience with bad headaches—all two of the real hangovers she'd ever had—she'd felt better after she'd eaten. Keeping her voice low and smooth in deference to his pain, she commented, "I hear Kato's a big storm."

No answer. Still feeling like crap, apparently.

He nibbled gingerly at the toast she set before him, gradually gaining enthusiasm for food. Before it was all said and done, he devoured all four of the slices. She toasted another batch of bread and grabbed a couple of pieces for herself before the human eating machine consumed the rest. The bacon finished cooking and she snagged a strip of it, setting the rest of it on the counter.

Mmm. Bacon. She couldn't remember the last time she'd indulged in its salty goodness. She nibbled at the slice, drawing out the experience for as long as she could. The kitchen was starting to smell like home. For a moment, she allowed herself to relish the memory of the big, warm kitchen back at the farm, redolent with the smells of bacon and biscuits and fresh milk.

She was surprised when Tom stood up and made his way around the breakfast bar. Bemused, she allowed him to shoo her away from the stove and even took the bar stool he indicated with the spatula he'd appropriated from her. In a combination of fond nostalgia and horror, she watched as Tom commenced scrambling eggs in the bacon grease. But when he pulled out the Cheez Whiz and sprayed a generous pile of it into the pan with the eggs, Madeline C. revolted entirely.

"You're actually going to eat those eggs?" she asked in distaste.

"Yup. So are you. They taste great this way."

"Have you got a defibrillator packed away in your pantry, then? Eat like that and you'll need it."

He shrugged. "If you get plenty of exercise and eat lots of

fresh fruits and vegetables, food like this won't hurt you. It's all about balancing the good with the bad."

Hmmppff. Might work for him, but no way could she eat like that. It had taken her endless grueling workouts and nibbling like a rabbit to get the figure she had now. No way was she blowing it on bacon grease and Cheez Whiz!

She watched Tom enthusiastically chow down his breakfast while she daintily consumed a piece of dry toast. At least, as the food filled his stomach, his face gradually took on a more pleasant expression. In fact, by the end of the meal, a definite glint was coming back into his eye. Uh-oh. She recognized that from last night. It might have been pitch-dark, but she'd still been able to make out that entirely male expression.

And darned if an answering flutter didn't leap to life in her stomach. No. No, no, no! Madeline C. was back in charge and she didn't jump into the sack with the Tom Larusos of the world. Period. End of discussion. She was holding out for a man who could give her security. Comfort. No worries. *Not* bacon and Cheez Whiz, darn it.

"So what's on the agenda for today besides getting you some stitches?" she asked, hoping to steer the conversation—and her errant urges to jump his bones—into safer waters.

He shrugged. "Delivering you to wherever you're staying, I suppose. Unless you'd rather wait out the storm here…"

And spend days on end stranded with him, alone, with nothing better to do than repeat last night's insanity over and over? Her breath actually caught for a moment at the idea. Oh, come on Maddie. Wake up and smell the Cheez Whiz. Belatedly, practical reality set in. Without the rush of having just escaped death, sex between them would be plain old, run-of-the-mill sex. And that she could definitely do without.

She mumbled, "Uh, my job…have to get back before the storm…"

Her company's A-list travel clients were always on the hunt for exclusive and private getaways in new and different places. And it was her job to scout out such retreats and review them. Paradise Cove had come highly recommended to her firm, so here she was, to check it out. Although, with a cyclone bearing down on Vanua Taru, she wasn't sure how good a look she was really going to get at the place.

If nothing else, she'd take a quick peek at the facilities. And, hey. She'd get a great firsthand look at the resort's evacuation procedures and customer service under duress. It wasn't ideal, but she would cut the place some slack in her write-up.

"C'mon," Tom said abruptly, startling her. "Let's go."

"Where are we going?" she blurted, stunned by her reluctance to end this relatively normal and companionable moment between them. After all, she'd never see him again after this. He'd crawl back into his bumlike existence and she'd return to the glitz and glamour of her real life, back in Chicago. Frigid, windy, gray Chicago, caught in the grip of winter's last arctic hurrah. For just an instant, she envied him for this carefree tropical existence. Even as she had the thought, the rain stopped outside and sun broke through, streaming through the big picture window and into the *bure,* filling it with cheerful light.

"We're going to town," Tom announced grimly.

Her pretravel research had shown there was a village on the island called Taru. It supposedly boasted local crafts, fresh, locally grown foods and a few high-end boutiques for the discriminating shopper…read, bored tourist with money burning a hole in his or her pocket. It sounded nice. Why, then, did Tom sound as if he'd rather have a root canal than go to Taru?

Perplexed, she followed him out onto the porch and looked around for some sort of conveyance. "How are we getting there?"

He glanced over at her in surprise. "Walking. It's only about a mile."

"A mile?" she exclaimed.

"Aww, c'mon. You do more than that on the treadmill every day."

Her gaze narrowed. "I prefer an elliptical machine."

He rolled his eyes.

She tried again. "I'm barefoot."

He glanced down at her toes, which suddenly developed a tendency to curl. "And?"

"I can't walk that far barefoot!"

He frowned. "Where are your shoes?"

"I lost them last night, of course."

He gave her a confused look, which, in turn, confused her. What was up with that? He was acting like the plane crash and their nearly dying had never happened.

"You can walk to town. I do it all the time. It is how Mother Nature designed us to get around."

"But I'll destroy my pedicure and...and...get blisters!"

"Heaven forbid," he retorted in mock horror.

It was her turn to glare at him. She'd forgotten just how taciturn and antisocial he could be. On the plane ride over here he'd hardly spoken two words to her—not until the crash and he'd yelled at her to bail out, and then, of course, pushed her out the door and scared a decade off her life. Jerk. Never mind that he'd saved her life. He was still a jerk.

Finally, she grumbled, "There had better be a decent boutique in Taru where I can stock up on makeup and clothes and shoes."

He didn't deign to reply, but merely took off walking down a one-person-wide sand path through the lush growth behind his villa. Thoroughly annoyed, she stalked after him. She'd worked for *months* after she moved to the city to soften her feet into their current cute, sexy condition. And all of that work was going to be destroyed in one half-hour hike.

After the rain, the strong noon sun heated the jungle into a steam bath that no doubt made her hair frizz up as if she'd stuck her finger in a light socket. She had undoubtedly sweated off all her makeup, too.

And after she'd worked so hard to improvise with a pot of gloss and some old mascara! It was a bloody miracle she'd managed to make herself look half-decent. But did he care? Noooo. Wasn't that just like a man, to totally not appreciate all the trouble she'd gone to in order to look good for him? She stomped along, taking out her frustration on the feckless sand beneath her feet.

Whoa. Rewind. Why was she fuming because she didn't look her best for Tom? She seriously didn't care what he thought of her looks. In fact, she hoped he thought she looked terrible. The more terrible the better, darn him! Making her traipse through the jungle like this, melting with heat and her clothes all sticky. Lord help her if her T-shirt was clinging to her as revealingly as Tom's was clinging to his bulging, sculpted, impressive back muscles....

Stop that.

The walk might be a mile, but through the soft sand, it felt like three. She was exhausted and drenched when the single row of traditional *bures* finally came into view. *This* was "town"? Great.

"This way," Tom directed.

"But I see a store over there."

He retorted shortly, "Shop later. Business first."

She scowled at his back. Did he have any idea how close to dying he was, coming between a desperate woman and her shopping like that?

"C'mon, slowpoke," he groused.

She'd liked him a *lot* better last night when they were crawling all over each other in their shock-induced sexual haze. She probably ought to be thankful he was showing his true colors like this. At least she would shed no crocodile tears when the two of them parted ways today. The sooner the better, in fact.

Roundly irritated, she minced across the hot asphalt of the village's lone street, cursing Tom with every blistering step. She cooled her heels in the strip of grass beside the road, then she marched after him to an unmarked building beyond the last shop. She stepped inside behind Tom's big, forbidding silhouette.

Oh, thank God. Cool air-conditioning wafted across her overheated skin. Civilization. At last. She closed her eyes and gave thanks to the electricity gods for their generous bounty.

When her head quit feeling like a hard-boiled egg about to explode and her face no longer felt tomato-red, she opened her eyes and took a look around. This place was built nearly identically to Tom's house, except the interior was outfitted as an office. The back half of the building was partitioned off by cubicle-style, partial walls.

The man seated at the desk just inside the door leaned back in his chair, with a not particularly pleased expression on his face as he gazed up at Tom. "What brings you in here, Laruso? Turning yourself in?"

"I'm here to report a crime," Tom replied evenly.

A glint of silver on the pocket of the man's tropical print shirt caught her attention as he tucked his thumbs in his belt and rocked his chair back on its hind legs. This must be the sheriff-cum-medic Tom hadn't wanted to see for his gash last night. Despite his casual pose, the guy's laconic expression suddenly wasn't nearly so laconic.

Tom spoke grimly. "Madeline, this is Herman Marquez, sheriff, mayor and resident EMT of Vanua Taru island. Herman, meet Madeline."

She smiled pleasantly at the sheriff. He had a competent air about him. Looked to be in his middle forties and had a nice smile.

"Tom forgot to mention that I'm also the public utilities commissioner, road maintenance man, pseudoveterinarian and volunteer fireman."

Her smile widened. "Do you fix toilets, too?"

"Yup. I'm a regular jack-of-all-trades."

"You must really have your hands full getting ready for this storm to hit, then."

Marquez's dark gaze clouded over with the myriad details obviously still in need of doing before Kato arrived. "Actually, I am rather busy. You're lucky you caught me at my desk. I was just on my way out."

Tom interrupted their exchange with a clearing of his throat. He sounded a tiny bit surly. Her eyebrow lifted faintly. Could it be? Was the strong, silent pilot jealous of the attention she was paying to sweet Herman? Would wonders never cease?

"Maddie—Madeline—and I were…taking in the view of the ocean last night…when we were attacked by a guy with a knife."

The sheriff's gaze swiveled to her in alarm, then back to Tom. His chair thumped to the floor. Abruptly, his eyes were grim and not the slightest bit laconic. "Tell me about it. Every-thing."

Tom complied emotionlessly. "We fell asleep on the beach. I don't know for how long. I woke up to the sound of someone approaching us. I wasn't…entirely alert…at the time."

Herman interrupted. "Drunk off your ass again, eh?"

Tom appeared unaffected by the jab. He continued as if the sheriff hadn't spoken. "The person attacked us with a knife. I rolled away from the initial strike and covered up Madeline, but I got scratched in the process. The guy ran away."

She interrupted with a snort. "Tom's got a big old slice across his back that needs stitches."

Marquez bolted to his feet at that, the EMT apparently subsuming the sheriff for the moment. "Lemme see," he ordered Tom.

Scowling at her, Tom shrugged out of his T-shirt. Maddie hovered protectively as the sheriff unwrapped her makeshift bandage and whistled. "Nice gash, buddy. The lady's right. That needs stitches. Lemme go get my suture kit."

Tom sighed in resignation and sat down on the edge of the guy's desk. Marquez was back in a moment. He spoke quietly to Tom. "I'd offer most patients a painkiller, but I think not for you."

She frowned. Huh? Tom just shrugged and didn't protest. She moved around in front of him so she didn't have to watch needles pierce his flesh.

"What can you tell me about the attacker?" Marquez asked as he commenced sewing up Tom's back.

Tom replied from between gritted teeth. "Male. Caucasian. Six feet tall. Athletic build. Maybe two hundred pounds, but no more. Light hair. It was too dark to see if it was blond or light brown."

The sheriff's mouth went nearly as tight as Tom's. "Sounds like the Sex on the Beach Killer."

"That's what Maddie said, too."

Given the way his lips were pressed together until they turned white and the way his fingers were digging into the side of the desk, Maddie refrained from correcting him aloud about her name. But she thought it in her head. She was Madeline C., darn it!

Herman's gaze swiveled to her apologetically over Tom's shoulder. "Then you two were…"

Tom answered quickly, "No. We were just lying there together in the sand."

Maddie winced. The way she vaguely recalled it, she'd been sprawled mostly on top of him and beginning to get some rather frisky ideas as she regained consciousness. It was sweet of Tom to edit the facts and protect her reputation like this.

"Anything else you can tell me about this attacker of yours?" Marquez asked intently.

Tom frowned. "He said something before he jumped us. I don't remember exactly what it was, but I remember being surprised by it. I think he called Madeline some sort of name. Something ugly."

Marquez nodded slowly. "An American FBI team is tracking this guy. They worked up a profile that suggests he's a woman hater. Has big hang-ups about sex. Were you two…uh…without clothes?"

Maddie's eyebrows shot up and her cheeks abruptly felt hot again. Tom replied dryly, "All but."

The sheriff nodded. "You said you were asleep. Perhaps in a position suggestive of…intimacy?"

Tom answered from between pain-gritted teeth, "When I woke up, Madeline was…uh…" he cast her an apologetic glance "…stretched out kind of, uh, across me. To a stranger, it would have looked more than a little suggestive."

Marquez swore under his breath and stepped back from Tom's back, surveying his work. "I gotta make some phone calls. Let the FBI boys know their killer may be here on Vanua Taru."

They waited while he placed a call and had a monotone, monosyllable conversation with the person at the other end. Marquez hung up the phone and looked over at both of them. "I'd appreciate it if you not spread it about that this guy may be on the island."

"Why not?" Maddie burst out, shocked. "People need to be warned!"

"Ma'am, we're about to be hit by a cyclone. Nobody's going to be down on the beaches messing around anyway. And I don't want to cause a panic when nobody can do anything to get away from this guy."

Tom moved his shoulders experimentally, then grimaced. "When he missed me with his knife, I jumped up with the intent to rip his head off. He took off and disappeared into the jungle. I think I scared him good. Maybe he'll go into hiding and not bug anyone for a while."

Marquez shook his head. "The profile says he's likely to be obsessive about secrecy. If he thinks you two have seen him and might be able to identify him, he'll need to take you both out."

Maddie stared in disbelief. She didn't even want to know what the sheriff meant by that. *Take them out?* As in permanently? She restrained an urge to squeak in dismay.

Tom said casually, "For all we know, he's already fled the island."

Marquez shook his head in the negative. "Nobody's gotten

on or off the island since sunset yesterday. Seas are too dangerous and flying conditions are too lousy." He threw Tom a withering look with that last phrase.

"We got onto the island after sunset," she piped up. "Of course we had to swim the last mile or two."

Both men turned to stare at her.

"What? When?" the sheriff and Tom asked simultaneously and incredulously.

Startled, she replied, "Our plane blew up just after sunset. I found Tom unconscious in the water and pulled him onto a piece of the debris that floated. Then I had to swim with Tom for what seemed like forever to get to shore. I'd guess it was a couple hours."

Both men talked over each other at once. *Blew up? How? Why? Where?*

She stared at Tom in disbelief. "Don't you remember it? We were hit by lightning and the engine caught on fire. You put the plane in a dive and it about shook us to pieces. At the last minute you leveled it off and told me to—"

"—bail out," he finished, partial comprehension lighting his dark eyes.

"So you do remember!" she exclaimed, relieved.

"Not entirely. But it explains a couple of images I had in a dream last night."

The sheriff swore under his breath as he reached for the phone. "And here I was already up to my elbows in crocodiles getting ready for a cyclone to strike and you had to go and drop this in my lap. What the hell were you doing flying in this lousy weather anyway?"

Tom glanced over at her, then back at Marquez. "She insisted. I told her it was suicide to try it, but she wouldn't listen."

She would've protested being painted as a bossy female

with a death wish, except he was mostly right. She'd just wanted to be done with this stupid trip to Fiji.

She, Alicia and Zoë had all leaped at the chance to review several world-class resorts in Fiji when their coworkers—known back at the office as the A-Team—had all contracted serious food poisoning at a sushi bar in Tokyo. The Secret Traveler Agency was due to put out a set of reviews of new and exclusive travel destinations for its wealthy and celebrity clients so they had called in Maddie, Alicia and Zoë to pinch-hit at the last second.

It was a great opportunity for the three of them to move up to the next level as travel reviewers, and they'd all been excited as they'd set out on this trip together. Of course, that had been before both Zoë and Alicia had crossed paths with this Sex on the Beach Killer. And they'd both had the good sense to get the hell out of Dodge already.

But she'd been determined to get the job done at all costs. It was a chance to prove herself to her employer, to demonstrate what a can-do girl she was. And to be honest, she'd also seen it as an opportunity to get a little ahead of Zoë and Alicia at the office. She liked both women well enough. In fact, she considered both of them good friends. But her under-riding sense of being a giant phony also gave her a bit of an inferiority complex at work. Zoë and Alicia were both beautiful, intelligent, sophisticated women, just like she wanted to be. She felt as if she had to work a little bit harder than they did to keep up. Hence, pressing a little too hard to get to Vanua Taru last night.

A disturbing thought occurred to her. If no one had gotten off the island since last night, how was she going to get out of there tonight like she'd planned? After all, she didn't want to get caught by the cyclone.

She asked the two men, "I'm going to be able to catch a ride of some kind out of here today, aren't I?"

Marquez replied without hesitation. "Not a chance. Everything's shut down until Kato passes through."

She stared at him in dismay. "But there's a killer loose on this island!"

He stared back at her grimly. "Let's sincerely hope not."

But they both knew darn good and well that she was right. They were trapped, all of them, on Vanua Taru with a vicious killer and a major cyclone blowing in.

Chapter 5

Tom had enough experience with both the FBI and crazies to fully believe the profiler if he said the killer would try to take out anyone who could identify him. He swore under his breath. Just what he needed. A killer gunning for him and Madeline. Frankly, this nutcase sounded out of Marquez's league altogether.

A year ago, he'd have been all over tracking this guy down on his own. But now...no way. Especially not with someone else's neck on the line, too. He glanced over at Maddie who, by the way, was as pretty today as she had been in the dark last night...although he liked her better completely without makeup. After their hike to town, only a little still clung to her skin, but it was enough to remind him of the rather unappealing plastic doll of a woman he'd picked up on the big island of Fiji yesterday afternoon.

Hey! Another memory! He remembered walking up to her

in an airport lounge and introducing himself. He also re-membered the thinly veiled disdain with which she'd perused his sloppy khaki Bermudas and casual polo shirt. It had chapped him a little, and the fact that he'd been bugged had bugged him even more. He was happy wallowing in his sorrows and his booze, and he didn't need the likes of her passing judgment on him.

He still didn't need her passing judgment on him. Although, he had to admit she hadn't been too judgmental last night in the dark when it was just the two of them. It was a novel sensation to be a comfort-sex guy that a woman would bed in private but wanted nothing to do with in public.

Tom forcibly unhunched his shoulders. The stitches knitted across his back hurt like hell. He could've used the painkiller the sheriff had withheld, but he understood the guy's decision. Tom was already well down the road to being a heavy substance abuser. No need to play with fire and expose him to narcotics.

And there was no need to expose Maddie to any further danger. Problem was, it would be a bitch to keep it away from her. Especially if Marquez was right and the killer was likely to try to murder the two of them.

A sinking feeling took hold of his gut.

Even if the sheriff and his men went after this Sex on the Beach Killer, Marquez only had a couple of part-time deputies at his disposal. The sheriff was a reasonably sharp guy, but neither he nor his compatriots had the training to handle a full-out serial killer. Add to that the fact that Marquez would have his hands full with crises related to the cyclone for the next week or two, and Tom saw the handwriting on the wall. He didn't even have to look at the sheriff to know what was coming next.

"I need you to do me a favor, Tom."

Nope. Didn't even need to hear the words. He *so* didn't want to go there. "No. No, no and…no!"

"Buddy, the statute of limitations has not run out for you on about twenty drunk and disorderlies, an assault charge or two and a couple more charges related to busting up Joe's bar. Stonewall me on this and I'm sure I can cook up a few dozen more to throw at you."

"Aww, c'mon, Herman. You know why I can't do this."

"Laruso, there's a cyclone coming. I've got a million and one things to do. And after the storm hits, me and the boys will have our hands full helping take care of folks and cleaning up. I need you to do this."

Maddie looked back and forth between them as if they were Martians speaking an alien tongue. Which was just as well. What she didn't know about how he'd spent the past six months was just as well.

The hell of it was that Herman was right. Reluctantly, he made eye contact with the sheriff. And did something he never did. Silently begged the man not to do this to him.

Marquez was implacable. "I need you to keep an eye on Miss Crummby."

Crummby? Her last name was Crummby? *Secret Traveler.* The name of the firm she worked for popped into his head all of a sudden. With the name came a few more details. She'd hired him to fly her to Vanua Taru and deliver her to Paradise Cove so she could stay there for a few days and write it up for the company's clients. He'd been sworn to secrecy over her identity and job. Whatever. But then, that meant…

His mind exploded with sudden realization. He hadn't picked her up and had a fling with her that landed them on the beach last night. He'd engaged in wild bunny sex with her on the assumption that it was a repeat perfor-mance…*but it hadn't been*. He'd just gotten in the panties of a *client*.

He swore long and hard inside his head.

His life might have gone completely to hell, and he might have let himself go completely to hell, but that didn't mean he'd abandoned his professional standards in the rare moments when he was actually still working. Hell, his stan-dards were all he had left.

Rule one: no drinking and flying.

Despite what Marquez thought, rule two: no drinking and fighting. He was too lethally trained for that to be fair to the other guy. And if he were being brutally honest with himself, he didn't trust his self-control enough not to seriously hurt or even kill someone if he mixed booze and violence. The only time he'd gotten in a fight here on Vanua Taru, he'd been sober. Hungover and grumpy as hell, but sober when a local kid decided to test him and see what the old man really had.

And last, but not least, rule number three: no messing around with his female clients. Ever. He cursed violently under his breath.

Marquez was talking again. "Look, Laruso. I don't like you. And I expect you don't much like me. But you and I both know your qualifications for this job, and frankly, they're better than mine."

Tom was surprised. It took a big man to admit something like that. Plenty of people wouldn't have been able to make such an admission. He nodded in silent acknowledgment, both of the truth of the statement and of the maturity it had taken to make it.

But to take on another protection job… Creeping dread climbed his spine one horrified vertebra at a time. He couldn't do it. He couldn't jump back into the arena. Especially not with another beautiful blond princess's life on the line.

"You got a gun, Laruso?"

He answered the sheriff absently as he fought down his panic attack with only limited success. "Yeah. Several."

"Keep one with you at all times. And keep it loaded, buddy. This Sex on the Beach Killer is a sick bastard...pardon me, ma'am."

Maddie nodded in what looked like abject terror. Tom was certain that wide-eyed shock in her eyes had nothing to do with hearing the word *bastard,* however. Maybe it had more to do with being stuck with a bastard—him—until this killer was caught. Hell, if she knew what was good for her, she'd be terrified at the thought.

In a last, desperate bid to escape this nightmare, Tom admitted the one thing he'd never said aloud before, never even barely allowed himself to think. "I lost the handle, Marquez. I'm afraid. Can't do it anymore. I lost one, and I can't lose another."

"Then catch the killer."

"Dammit!" Tom exploded. "Don't you understand what I'm saying? I've been sitting on my ass for months, drinking myself to sleep at night, not working out. My reflexes are shot, I'm in crappy shape. Hell, I can't even hold my hand steady enough to shoot." As evidence of that last, he held out his right hand, which was, indeed, shaking. With pure, unadulterated terror.

The sheriff slapped him on the shoulder. "Time to crawl out of the bottle and rejoin the living, old man."

"But—"

"The way I hear it, you functioning at fifty percent is better than most lawmen operating at full capacity. You're not wiggling out of this, so get over it and get on with it. Consider this your penance for past sins."

Tom staggered backward. Actually, physically staggered. An image of Arielle's mutilated body flashed into his mind's eye. No amount of penance could make up for that failure. None. He looked over at Maddie in mute appeal. "Don't let him do this to you…"

She frowned. "I don't know what's going on, but I know I want to get off this island. Can you do that for me?"

He latched on to the idea like a drowning man grabbing a life preserver. "That's a great idea! I'll fly you out right away—"

"Sorry," Marquez interrupted. "Aren't you forgetting that your plane is at the bottom of the ocean?"

"I'll borrow someone else's."

"Yeah, right. And one of the other pilots is gonna let you fly their plane in this weather. Seas are running thirty to forty feet above normal and the winds are gusting up to sixty knots. No floatplane can take off or land that. You're not flying anywhere until Kato passes."

Tom closed his eyes against the despair overwhelming him. Damn, damn, damn. "When's the storm gonna be over?"

"The main cyclone should hit tomorrow, late morning. The eye is forecast to pass over late afternoonish. Then the back side of the storm. Two, maybe three days, all told."

Tom swore under his breath. Three days to guard a principal around the clock by himself? Even when he was in top form, that would have been a bitch of an assignment.

The sheriff said grimly, "Precisely because of your past history, you'll protect her better than anyone else on the island could." A pause. And then Marquez added quietly, "Including me."

The two of them had been butting heads for months. It couldn't have been easy for Marquez to ask him for help. No easier than it was for him to admit that Marquez was right.

He exhaled heavily. "What can you tell me about this Sex on the Beach Killer?" If he was going to have to protect Maddie from the bastard, he might as well learn everything he could about the guy. Knowledge was perhaps the most crucial ingredient in keeping a subject safe, particularly knowledge of any threats to the subject.

Marquez surprised him by slapping a nearly six-inch-tall pile of folders down on the desk. "Here's everything I've got."

Tom eyed the stack. Then he eyed Madeline, who shifted impatiently even as he glanced at her. It would take him hours to even skim through the files, let alone study them thoroughly. She wasn't going to like sitting on the bench in the corner and cooling her heels while he combed through this monster pile of paperwork.

"Can I take this home to read?" Tom asked in deep resignation.

"Yeah, sure. I've been through it so many times I've about got it memorized." Marquez laughed shortly. "Besides, it ain't like I'm gonna have time to look at it in the next few days."

"Herman, could you or one of your boys escort Madeline down to Trudi's place? She lost her luggage in the crash last night. She might like to do a little shopping while I take a preliminary glance at this stuff. And I don't want her alone."

The sheriff sighed. "I don't have time for it, but I'll run her down. I suppose I owe you that. The summary file's on top. Take a look at that first."

Tom nodded tersely while Madeline, who'd perked up considerably at the mention of shopping, wasted no time heading for the door.

Before the sheriff followed Maddie out the door, Tom

pulled out his still damp wallet, which had somehow managed to stay tucked in his back pocket all through last night's ordeal. He passed Marquez a credit card to cover Maddie's purchases. After all, she'd saved his life. It was the least he could do to say thank-you. And, if it kept her out of his hair and from turning into a "I-have-nothing-to-wear" harpy, he was all for financing a shopping trip. He didn't think he'd ever seen Arielle wear the same outfit twice. And she'd been worse than a harpy when she didn't get her shopping on.

The sheriff paused in the doorway. "Find this guy, Laruso. Capture him or ki—" Marquez broke off. "*Whatever* it takes. Just stop him. You get my meaning?"

Tom heard the guy loud and clear. He was green-lighted to kill this psycho if need be and no questions would be asked about the circumstances of the takedown. He nodded grimly, his gut in a hopeless twist. "I hear ya. Loud and clear."

"Thanks, Tom."

"Yeah, sure. And Marquez?"

"Yeah?"

"You're a sonofabitch."

Laughing heartily, the sheriff slapped his tan cowboy hat on his head and walked out of the building, leaving Tom alone to ponder the dossier of the man he was supposed to hunt down and kill.

Maddie stepped into the boutique, housed in yet another wood and thatch structure and gasped in delight. It might not be Rodeo Drive, but it was crammed wall-to-wall with a selection and quality of goods that rivaled anything Beverly Hills had to offer. Trudi turned out to be a German expatriate who'd moved to Vanua Taru some twenty years previously and had opened this shop to cater to the resort crowd. And, oh, how she catered. After Trudi agreed to close the shop and lock the doors behind him, Sheriff Marquez left to tend to other things and the two women dived into power shopping with gusto.

Maddie picked out beach casual wear, a little, black Versace cocktail dress from the recent Milan collection and a barely there bikini that made her think of Tom. She added lingerie, designer cosmetics and hair-care products and even several pairs of crashingly expensive shoes to the growing pile. She figured she deserved a treat after yesterday's ordeal and having to be seen in public in nothing more than a man's T-shirt. Her one consolation was that Tom's shirt didn't have a beer logo on it.

Trudi served her a light lunch of fresh tuna fillets, a pineapple and coconut salad to die for and mango white-wine spritzers. Trudi even offered to give her a quick manicure. By the time the German woman was done pampering her, Maddie felt almost fully human. She made a mental note to mention Trudi's shop in her review.

She asked her hostess, "Can I buy a cell phone on this island? I lost mine yesterday." Some octopus was probably having a great time running up text-messaging charges with it at this very moment.

"Not here. Besides, once Kato hits, the phone tower will go down."

"You mean it'll lose power?"

"No," the woman said and laughed. "I mean it'll blow over. Fall down."

Maddie lurched in alarm. "Just how bad is this storm supposed to be?"

Trudi shrugged. "Depends on how direct a hit we take and which side of the eye we end up on."

"What are the weather reports saying?"

Trudi replied, "We're hoping the worst of it slides north of the island. But we are expecting close to a direct hit."

And there was a killer running around on the loose. Who Tom was apparently going to try to catch. "Trudi, what's the latest on the Sex on the Beach Killer?"

"They haven't caught him. It has been two weeks since he killed anyone. Folks are saying it's about time for him to strike again."

Maddie closed her eyes for a pained moment. She didn't care what the sheriff and Tom said. She was warning this kind woman. "I was just over at the sheriff's office, and he has reason to believe the killer might be here on Vanua Taru. Be careful, will you, Trudi?"

The woman laughed off the warning. "It's not like I'm planning on going down to the beach and making whoopee at my age. I never could stand to get sand down my knickers, anyway. I'll be safe enough, don't you worry, now. Besides, after that last murder got so much publicity, I don't think anybody's going to be fooling around on beaches anywhere in the South Pacific until this weirdo's caught, sweetie."

Trudi cleared away their lunch plates and moved over to the cash register. She started ringing up the purchases as it dawned on Maddie that, along with her cell phone, her purse and its entire contents were also sitting on the bottom of the ocean right about now.

"Oh, no!" she exclaimed. "I don't have any way to pay for all this. I know my credit-card number, though. Could we call my company and verify my card or something?"

The German woman waved a breezy hand. "Not to worry. Tom Laruso is picking up the tab."

Maddie stared. Felt her face go red hot. Tom was paying

for all her new clothes? It felt suspiciously like payment for services rendered last night. And she didn't like the feeling one bit. Give a guy sex and get a lavish shopping spree, huh?

Something cynical in the back of her head muttered, *And that's not what you'll be doing when you marry for money? Keep the rich husband happy and in return, help yourself to his wealth and security?* A bitter taste accumulated on her tongue.

Trudi startled her by laughing knowingly and announcing, "The local girls will be plenty disappointed that you've landed Vanua Taru's most eligible bachelor. They've been eyeing him for months. Heck, if I thought he'd pay attention to a woman ten years older than him for more than a second, I'd be after him myself. That boy's hot. Even if he does drink a little too much now and then. But that's nothing a good woman couldn't cure him of quick enough. I figure he's just lonely."

Maddie closed her eyes, mortified. As soon as word got out that he'd paid for this elaborate shopping spree—and she knew without a shadow of a doubt that it would—her reputation would be in shreds. Except ultimately, who would know? This was a dinky little island in the middle of nowhere. She could stand the leers of the locals for a day or two until she could get off this godforsaken rock.

"How long will it be until transportation off the island is restored?" Maddie asked in resignation.

Trudi shrugged. "A week. Maybe two. Depends on the damage and how fast the storm passes. The worse the damage is, the faster we'll get relief flights and boats."

Great. Either pray for a natural disaster and a quick escape or put up with a killer stalking her—and the bodyguard that came with the killer.

Please, Lord, wipe this island out!

Chapter 6

"Feeling better?"

A thrill raced through Maddie at the sound of Tom's rich voice behind her. She turned around, modeling a flirty silk camisole and miniskirt ensemble for him. It floated around her, whispery light. One of the spaghetti straps slipped off her shoulder, and she ran a freshly manicured fingernail underneath it to slide it back up. She noticed Tom's hungry gaze on the movement, and she couldn't resist making a slow tease of it.

What *was* it about this guy? She never threw herself at men. She was the ice queen, the unassailable goddess that men panted over and chased down. At least that was the idea. Every how-to book she'd ever read on landing the perfect husband was clear on that point. Make the guy come to you. Never, ever, be the one doing the chasing.

Of course, the good news was that Tom Laruso was emphatically not marriage material. He definitely fell into the category of fun for the moment, but don't brag about him to your friends.

"This your haul?" he asked casually, gesturing at the row of glossy shopping bags lined up by the counter.

She glanced down at the bags in chagrin. Maybe she'd gone a little overboard on his credit card. "As soon as I get new credit cards and checks issued to me, I'll pay you back."

He waved a negligent hand. "Don't worry about it. You've more than earned it, sweetheart."

Trudi's carefully plucked eyebrows shot practically past her perfectly highlighted hairline. Maddie's cheeks burst into flame—that was how they felt at any rate. She peeked over at Tom to see if he was even vaguely aware of what he'd just insinuated.

The cad was smirking.

Fat cat swallowed the canary, knew damn well what he'd just implied, *smirking.*

Her gaze narrowed. Two could play that game. She purred, "Baby cakes, you really shouldn't have. I'm sure you'll be able to…" she paused for dramatic effect "…perform…next time. You didn't have to buy me all this stuff to apologize."

She wasn't sure whose jaw dropped farther, Tom's or Trudi's. Time to go for the kill. "After all," she continued, waving a negligent hand in blithe dismissal, "a man your age…these things are bound to happen. Fortunately, I hear that some of the new medications for it are working wonders."

Hoo baby. Good thing she wasn't planning on spending any more time with this guy after he delivered her to Paradise Cove. He looked about ready to do her serious bodily harm. Thankfully, he was going to be busy running around the island chasing after the Sex on the Beach nutcase while she did a quickie site survey of the resort before Kato arrived.

While she vacillated between unholy amusement and alarm at what she'd just done, Tom did the weirdest thing. He shut down. She couldn't think of any other way to describe it. His face went completely blank and all expression whatsoever drained from his eyes. It was as if the man just went away, leaving a cold, hard automaton standing in his place. She expected him to break out any second with a deadpan, "Just the facts, ma'am."

Instead, he scooped up all the bags with smooth efficiency and coolly said, "I'll be outside whenever you're ready to go."

Even Trudi looked perplexed at his sudden personality shutdown. "You take care of yourself, Madeline. You'll be nice and safe over at the resort. My husband worked on it when it was built, God rest his soul, and they constructed it to withstand bigger storms than this."

Maddie nodded, bemused, and took the receipt for her purchases. She winced at the total. Her current bank-account balance wouldn't cover it, but she could pay Tom with a credit card and then chip away at the debt for the next few months. Of course, she'd have to severely curtail her incidental expenses for some weeks to come.

It was a painful reminder of why she'd embarked on the whole Madeline C. project in the first place. She was determined not to live out her life in the backbreaking, spirit-breaking, relentless financial uncertainty in which she'd grown up. She told herself fiercely that she wasn't so cold-hearted as to plan to marry purely for money. But if she did eventually fall in love and marry, why not do it with a rich guy?

This chance to hang out at high-dollar resorts was perfect

for meeting the right kind of man. She'd be a fool to blow such a golden opportunity by getting hung up on a fling with Tom Laruso, when Mr. Right might be here at this very moment, waiting for her.

She stepped outside, and the afternoon's muggy heat hit her like a brick wall. Even in the uncertain sunshine the humidity made breathing difficult. In a matter of seconds, she felt her carefully applied makeup making like a goose and migrating south toward her chin. *There's nothing like the feel of your face melting to know it's hot outside.*

The latest band of thunderstorms had spun past, leaving the island in a gap before the next spiral band of bad weather moved in. Tom lounged in the driver's seat of a covered golf cart, her bags already stashed behind him.

"Are we going golfing?" she asked in surprise.

"Small island. Gasoline has to be shipped in and gets pricey. Solar cells recharge electric carts for free."

She climbed in the seat beside him. Crud. He was back to his irascible, untalkative self of the day before. Her and her big mouth. She'd liked him a lot better when he was relaxed and open with her, before she'd made the wisecrack impugning his sexual performance.

"Look, Tom. I'm sorry about what I said. I was just joking around. Really, I didn't mean anything by it. It's just that, in the circles I run in, you either go on the offensive or expect to be the brunt of the jokes."

He spared her only the briefest of glances. "Maybe you need to get new friends."

She smiled ruefully. "Those are the new friends."

He made no comment. She noticed his gaze scanning all around continuously as he drove down an asphalt strip barely wide enough to qualify as a road. As they left the village, the jungle pressed in around them and over them, creating a living tunnel of green. She expected Tom to relax once they were under the cover of the foliage, but if anything, he waxed even more tense.

"Everything okay?" she asked cautiously.

"Just doing my job."

"Staring at the trees?"

He grunted. "The good news is this guy's partial to knives."

"And that's good news, why?"

"He's less likely to shoot us."

"Shoot us?" she exclaimed. "What for?"

He glanced over at her long enough to frown. "You heard the sheriff. The Sex on the Beach Killer thinks we saw him. He has to kill us now."

"Well, yeah. But if we stay off the beach and don't mess around in a public place, everything will be okay, won't it?"

"What the sheriff meant was, if necessary, this guy will depart from his usual mode of killing to silence us. What *I* meant was that I doubt he brought a gun with him to the island, and I also doubt he's had time to secure himself one since last night. But, don't kid yourself. He *will* try to kill us. And *that's* why I'm watching the trees."

Funny, but she suddenly developed a burning need to watch trees, too. Or rather the spaces between them. The jungle's underbrush wasn't nearly as dense as she'd pictured it. Ferns and flowering bushes carpeted the jungle floor, and a surprisingly wide variety of trees created a lush canopy overhead. She became aware of the smell of the place, fresh and alive, with a faint overlay of exotic spices.

The cart rounded a bend and she gasped in delight. A magnificent water garden unfolded before her, with flowing waterfalls and dancing fountains creating rainbow sprays across the interlinking pools. Red, oriental temple-shaped towers rose out of the pools, and quaint pavilions dotted small islands among the ponds. To say it was magnificent didn't even begin to do the expansive garden justice.

"Wow," she breathed.

Tom commented, "Take a good look now. The cyclone will wipe it out. They'll have to rebuild this more or less from scratch."

She looked more closely and spied a pair of gardeners tipping over one of the temple statues and passing it to more workers on shore. She heartily hoped they could save most of the major garden elements before the storm.

Tom followed the driveway around the garden to a spacious hotel lobby built in the open-air Balinese style. Impressed, she stepped out of the cart and walked into the spacious atrium, admiring the intricate carvings covering the giant logs overhead that made up the structure's framework. Cool air blew down on her from somewhere, driving back the muggy afternoon heat and giant pots of greenery and tropical foliage gave the place a comfortable, welcoming feel.

A man in white linen pants and a turquoise polo shirt greeted them and Tom made the introductions. Maddie recognized the name Nigel Cumberland. He was the resort's general manager. "Miss Crummby, welcome to Paradise Cove," Nigel said in a British-accented voice.

He was around six feet tall, trim and handsome. Made a good first impression for the resort.

"I'm afraid you haven't caught us at our best, Miss Crummby. Unfortunately, I fear you won't get to fully enjoy our amenities."

She smiled warmly. "I'm just glad to have gotten here before the storm, even if I can only see this place at its best for one day. I heard it was gorgeous, and that's very true."

Nigel smiled warmly. "We'll do our best to make you comfortable in what little time there is before the cyclone hits. And I assure you, our storm shelter is second to none. You'll be perfectly safe with us."

He actually sounded calm about the approaching cyclone. Score one for Nigel and company.

"If you'll step into my office for a moment, Miss Crummby, I have a bit of paperwork for you. Sheriff Marquez rang me up a little while ago and filled me in on your mishap last night."

Frowning, she followed him. This was not a typical hotel check-in—and she should know. She'd done dozens of them in the past year. Nigel sat down at his desk and gestured for her to have a seat across from him. He passed a thin file over to her.

"Am I correct in guessing that you've lost all of your identification, money and credit cards?"

She nodded.

He continued, "I took the liberty of contacting your bank, and they've wired you emergency funds—which you'll find in the white envelope—traveler's checks in the amount of two thousand U.S. dollars. Also, they faxed me a document…" He leaned across to fish out a printed form and pointed for her to see. "If you'll sign here, I've filled out a travel insurance claim on your behalf and only need your signature to complete it. I'll fax it back to your carrier in a moment."

Stunned at his efficiency, Maddie nodded and signed where he pointed.

Nigel continued, "Within the week, ten thousand dollars of travel insurance monies will be deposited in your checking account by your credit card company. If you have any other personal travel insurance, you will need to file that claim yourself when you return home. The American Embassy in

Suva is working up a temporary passport for you. It will be ready in three days. Best I could do with a cyclone coming. But, they agreed to courier it over to Nadi and have it waiting for you at the International Airport. Oh, and your airline tickets have been replaced and will also be waiting for you in Nadi when you're ready to fly home to Chicago."

Numb with shock, Maddie signed the remaining papers he placed before her. She looked up at the British man. "Where can I get one of you to take home with me?"

He smiled, a dashing grin that all but rolled her socks down. "In my experience, the character of a person—or an institution—is most evident in times of crisis. It is our pleasure here at the Cove to help you."

If his observation was true, then what did jumping Tom's bones last night say about her character? She was afraid to look over at him with that thought foremost in her mind.

Nigel got up from his desk and poured them all glasses of ice water. As he handed a crystal tumbler to Tom, he commented, "You're looking good, mate."

"You mean I'm looking sober?"

Maddie looked back and forth between them as the two men traded grins. Obviously buddies. Hard to picture the suave Brit and the scruffy American having anything in common.

Nigel said, "Don't be a stranger around here, Tom. I said you're welcome at the Cove as my guest anytime, and I meant it."

Tom replied with what sounded like genuine regret, "I didn't want to bring down your property values. You never know when there's a resort reviewer lurking nearby."

She glared at Tom, and he grinned back unrepentantly. He turned back to Nigel. "Marquez is forcing me to clean up my act whether I want to or not."

"Blighter!" Nigel exclaimed.

"Bastard," Tom agreed fervently.

Maddie rolled her eyes. No matter what the nationality or culture, male bonding was the same the world over.

"If you'll follow me, Miss Crummby, we've left your villa open. The cyclone shouldn't arrive until tomorrow, so you can spend at least one day in paradise."

The walk to the villa was nearly as magnificent as the water gardens, with an artfully naturalized tropical garden on her left and the ocean below on her right. Nigel pointed out various native plants and birds along the way.

They arrived at a spacious *bure* not unlike Tom's. As Nigel unlocked the door, he apologized, "I'd put you in a villa down on the beach, but the main storm surge is due in late tonight. I didn't want to take a chance on you getting flooded out."

Maddie laughed. "Gee, thanks. I've had enough unplanned dips in the ocean for one lifetime already on this trip."

She noted Tom's momentary frown. It looked as if he'd just remembered something. Maybe a snippet of that god-awful swim for shore had come back to him.

"Stay here with Nigel," Tom bit out. He disappeared inside the *bure* while the Brit slipped behind her, placing himself squarely between her and the jungle.

"Let me guess. You're some sort of fancy bodyguard, too."

"Ex-bobby, miss."

"Ex-what?"

"British police. Scotland Yard. I don't have anywhere near the personal security expertise that your man does, but I picked up a bit here and there."

"Tom's that good?" she asked in surprise.

"He was. Until Arielle."

She opened her mouth to ask more, but Tom appeared in the doorway behind her. "All clear."

"In you go, then," Nigel said cheerfully. "Tea's at four. Dinner at seven. I'm afraid the menu will be somewhat limited tonight. The kitchen staff has been a wee bit occupied preparing and storing nonperishable food for the next week."

Tom spoke up. "Anything I can do to help you around here?"

The Brit shook his head. "We've got things well in hand. All my disaster-preparedness training finally came in handy after all."

With a pleasant nod, he strode off down the path, leaving Tom and Maddie alone on the porch.

"Let's get you under cover," Tom murmured.

She frowned and stepped into the villa. It was lovely, but lacked the character of Tom's place. "Aren't you supposed to be running around the island looking for the Sex on the Beach Killer?"

He shrugged. "No need to run around."

Foreboding flooded her. "Why not?"

"He'll come to me."

"He will?" Alarm—and something else dangerous and breathless that she didn't care to examine too closely—raced through her. "How?"

"He'll come to *us*, actually. Marquez gave me two jobs to do. First, he told me to keep you safe. Second, he told me to catch the killer. The only way to pull off both of those assignments is to stick by you until the killer shows up and then grab him."

The killer…come to them? "You're kidding." Cold terror stole her breath away.

"Do I look like I'm kidding?"

She studied him closely. He looked like he needed a shave.

He looked tired. And he looked distinctly more focused than before their visit to town. A certain grim set about his mouth was new, too. Nope, not kidding. He looked dead serious.

"How close are you planning on sticking to me?" she asked cautiously.

"Like glue."

Glue? A distinctly sexual flutter tickled her innards. She told herself sternly that there would be no repeats of last night. That had been an anomaly, born of nearly dying and the crazy rush of having survived. She was calm now. In control. And so was he. This sticking like glue bit would be all right.

She nodded belatedly. "Okay. Until the killer's caught."

Tom set down her bags, and she hung up her clothes neatly in the closet, lining up each pair of shoes just so under the outfit they went with. As a kid, she'd never owned more than two pairs of shoes at a time—one pair of tennis shoes and one pair of school/church shoes. Of course, she had a clunky pair of rubber boots that came nearly to her knees for when she mucked out the barns, but those hardly counted as shoes. It was no surprise, then, that Madeline C. delighted in frivolous, flirty and downright un-sensible shoes.

When the stilettos, espadrilles and sandals were arranged to her satisfaction, she looked up and asked reflectively, "When you say, 'Like glue,' are we talking at the same resort, or within shouting distance?"

"We're talking within kissing distance," he replied as dry as the desert. In summer. In a drought.

Oh, my.

They both slept through tea. But after the night they'd had last night, it was no surprise to Tom. He allowed himself the nap on the assumption that the killer a) didn't know where they were yet and b) wouldn't have the *cajones* to strike in broad daylight. Besides, he and Maddie both were going to get precious little sleep over the next several days if he didn't miss his guess. Between the killer and the storm, they needed to stock up on all the rest they could get now.

He was just as happy to shack up in the *bure* and order room service, assuming it was still operating. Maddie, however, was having no part of that. For a woman who ate like a rabbit—an anorexic one at that—she was surprisingly adamant when she woke up that she needed a real meal tonight. Thank goodness. He'd seen some pretty whacky diets during his years in the celebrity security business. The whole business of starvation and fad diets had always bugged him.

While Maddie disappeared into the bathroom to dress for supper, he eyed the fully stocked bar in the corner of the living room askance. He wasn't getting the shakes or uncontrollably restless, but he felt a definite craving for a shot of scotch. Rule two, dammit. He was not mixing firearms and alcohol and that's all there was to it.

Not only was Maddie's neck on the line here, but so was his. If the killer had any sense at all, he'd be more interested in killing the big, athletic man who'd seen his face and had been prepared to fight him off than the tiny, weak woman who would be easy prey as soon as her companion was picked off. It was a novel sensation, being the primary target of a stalker for a change. Usually, he was only an annoying obstacle to be gotten around or passed through. That anonymity had helped him do his job, in fact. But now, he felt…exposed.

As recently as two days ago, he'd frankly have shrugged at the prospect of getting killed. Maybe even would've welcomed the idea on some unconscious level.

But now, with a job to do—and face it, with the booze-induced haze of the past few months beginning to lift—he was suddenly much less interested in dying. He wondered sardonically if the great sex with Maddie was the cause of that. He snorted to himself. Better not confess that to her or she'd be insufferable from now till kingdom come.

Maybe it was the challenge of the woman herself that was restoring his will to live. Her quick wit and quicker tongue were certainly keeping him on his toes.

She emerged from the bathroom and he did a sharp double take. The little black dress was simple, but it clung to her in all the right places. Her hair and makeup were perfect. He had to admit, she looked pretty damned good gussied up like that. Had she gone to all that trouble for him? Momentary warmth spread through his gut at the idea. But then reality intruded upon the concept. She was probably only concerned with the resort's dinner dress code. A pang of regret stabbed him. It would have been nice if she'd done it for him, though.

"Still hungry?" he asked. In his experience, women who stood in front of mirrors for too long tended to lose their appetites.

"Starving." Her gaze raked down him as if he was the main course for dinner, shooting an answering shudder of lust through him. "Is that what you're going to wear?" she asked neutrally.

Too neutrally. He glanced down at his black Bermuda shorts and black Hawaiian shirt with its understated royal blue print. For him, this was pretty damned dressed up. As his tan could attest to, he'd barely seen the inside of a shirt since he'd arrived in Fiji. No doubt about it. He'd turned into a bum.

He drawled. "Hello. *Black* shorts and Hawaiian shirt. Evening wear."

She didn't say anything, but her tacit disapproval was evident. Tough. The big city girl could get over her silly ideas on proper clothing and count herself lucky that he was wearing any clothes at all…or that she was still wearing hers, for that matter. That dress was positively calling to him to strip it off her.

As they set out for the main lodge, the foolishness of her clothing rapidly became apparent, her shoes in particular. Her spike heels caught between the path's pavers, and she ended up having to cling to his arm for dear life or else risk breaking an ankle. Not that he was complaining about the clinging part, of course.

After a few minutes of walking with her plastered to him from shoulder to knee, he murmured, "Switch sides, will you?"

"Am I drooling on your shoulder?"

He laughed. "No. I want you on the ocean side where there's less threat, and when we approach the lodge, I want my shooting hand free."

Her face clouded over, but there wasn't anything he could do about it. Fact was, a threat lurked out there somewhere, and they'd be suicidal to ignore it.

In the prematurely gathering dusk of another line of storms, he walked Maddie up to the main facility. Unlike her, he knew what was coming and wasn't taken aback at the formality of the main dining room. He had to give Nigel credit. They were one day from a hurricane, yet the white linen tablecloths were still starched within an inch of their lives, the crystal still spotless and the cuisine as exquisite as ever.

Okay, so he did feel a little weird walking into a four-star gourmet restaurant in shorts. Once upon a time he'd owned a whole closet full of suits, and even a custom-made tuxedo that lay correctly over a concealed shoulder holster. He wouldn't have minded dressing up for Maddie if he'd had any of his old clothes with him. But he hadn't been thinking that far ahead when he'd tossed a few things in an overnight bag, not after the curveball Marquez had lobbed at him this morning. Fortunately, many of the guests tonight were also dressed down as they made their last preparations to ride out Kato.

What did take Tom totally by surprise about the meal was watching Maddie eat. Oh, she consumed her food as politely as the next person, daintily even. But with each bite, she would close her eyes and savor the taste on her tongue for a moment before she swallowed. By the third course, he was about ready to drag her under the table and have his way with her. No way was he making it through four more courses. His shorts felt way too tight, and he was distinctly overheated about the gills before she duly savored and consumed the last bite of her berry-custard flan.

"Let's go for a walk," he growled.

She nodded blissfully and followed him from the restaurant in a practically postcoital fog. Damn. He might have to take up gourmet cooking if great food did this to women!

He guided her down to the beach, and her head swiveled every which way, taking in the terraced gardens dotting the steep hillside leading down to the white sand. Little gasps of delight escaped her lips now and then, and it was all he could do not to ravish her on the spot. High tide was in, and most of the beach was swallowed by pounding waves. The surf wasn't bad, with waves down here on the south shore, out of the brunt of the arriving storm, running between ten and twelve feet. But the waves rolled in heavily and continuously. Definitely some serious energy building up offshore.

He waited while she kicked her shoes off and dangled

them in her fingertips. Then, as they stepped out onto the beach, he draped his arm across her shoulders. Gratifyingly, she reciprocated and readily twined her arm around his waist. The profile on the Sex on the Beach Killer said he was attracted to and repulsed by public displays of affection... probably a result of some sort of childhood trauma involving pornography.

Tom sincerely hoped he and Maddie didn't have to resort to public pornography to draw the guy out, but something along those lines seemed like the most efficient way to get this guy to show himself. He'd really love to nab the bastard before Cyclone Kato got here. That way, he could tuck Maddie into a storm shelter, go back home and retreat into a nice, safe bottle of scotch to ride out the storm.

They strolled along the widest stretch of beach, but no weirdo with a knife leaped out and confronted them. They stopped near the steps leading back up to the lodge. The latest line of thunderstorms had broken and sunset bled across the turbulent ocean, creating a spectacular tableau at their feet.

He couldn't bring himself to ruin the moment by jumping Maddie's bones, so he settled for drawing her back against his chest and propping his chin lightly on the top of her head while they watched the sunset together. With her high heels off, she was a tiny little thing. Made him feel...protective. Must be the old instincts of his job starting to come back.

As the last vestiges of twilight faded from the sky, Maddie looked around nervously. Why he persistently thought of her as Maddie and not Madeline, even as brightly polished as she was now, he couldn't really say. The one name just seemed to fit her and the other seemed wrong, somehow.

"Shouldn't we go inside where the bad guy can't get a clear shot at us?" she asked.

"On the contrary. That's the whole point of being out here. We *want* to attract his attention."

"You don't have any idea where or who he is, though."

He shrugged. "We know he's around six feet tall and Caucasian, which means he won't pass for a native of Vanua Taru. Of the Caucasian transplants to the island, everyone who lives here recognizes each other on sight. So, our killer has to hide among the tourists, or he'll be spotted in a second. And there's only one resort on this little island. Our guy has to be here at Paradise Cove." And as he uttered the words, he knew in his gut they had to be true.

Abruptly, he felt the killer's presence nearby. Another old instinct roaring back to life? Had his famous intuition finally returned? Although in all fairness, it hadn't ever really left him. He'd *told* Arielle not to go out that night. He'd had one of his gut feelings that something very bad was going to happen, and he'd shared it with her. She'd just laughed, and then disobeyed him and snuck out without any guards—and died.

"I don't like it out here," Maddie announced. "I feel… naked."

He bit back a snappy comeback about wishing she was. He was reluctant to go out of his way to make her mad, even if her snarky comment at Trudi's place did deserve a bit of revenge. Amusement rippled through him. Failure to perform…hah! She hadn't had any complaints about his performance last night!

That hadn't been good sex, or even great sex they'd had. It had been epic, mind-blowing, out-of-this-world sex. He could seriously go for more of that— *Hold on, there, big guy.* She was now the client again, thanks to Sheriff Marquez. *Note to self: strangle Marquez the next time I see him.*

Paradise Cove was, indeed, built on a cove, a teardrop-shaped affair rimmed by the whitest, smoothest sand beaches he'd ever seen. They walked all the way to the southeast point of the cove, and Tom helped Maddie climb the boulder-strewn promontory to view the ocean beyond as night fell and stars winked into the sky.

"Wow," she breathed.

From there, they caught glimpses of the pale arc of the island's barrier reef, mostly obscured by the beginnings of Kato's storm surge. Beyond it, the Pacific Ocean heaved, magnificent and endless, stirred by Poseidon's angry hand.

Maddie shivered as the full force of the wind—around forty knots and gusting higher—whipped at her dress, plastering it to her lithe body. She really did have a great figure.

"Cold?" he murmured.

"A little. But I'm glad you brought me up here. This is incredible. There's nothing even remotely like this where I come from."

"I dunno. Lake Michigan is pretty fierce sometimes. They don't call Chicago the *Windy City* for nothing."

"I'm not from Chi—" She broke off, if he wasn't mistaken, in embarrassment.

"Where are you from?" he asked, curious to know why that odd note had entered her voice.

"Manhattan, actually."

Ah. That explained the sharp-tongued humor. But New York City? He'd lived there on and off for years, chasing his clients around in pursuit of exclusive shopping and publicity exposure. Maddie didn't strike him as a Big Apple girl. Something indefinably...New York...was missing in her. He was definitely off his game at people-reading where she was concerned.

She shivered a little more noticeably, and he used it as an excuse to draw her close to his side. She snuggled up against him greedily, trying to absorb even more warmth from him. Perfect. They looked just like a pair of lovers, out enjoying the evening before finding someplace secluded to engage in plenty of hot sex.

Are you looking, you crazy sonofabitch? Do you see us? We're climbing all over each other here. Come out, come out, wherever you are…

The man adjusted his binoculars to bring the couple into sharper focus, crawling all over each other right out in the open for all the world to see. He used the zoom feature to bring the couple's faces into plain view…and stared, stunned. Rage simmered low in his gut, building quickly into a boiling cauldron of molten fury.

Had they learned *nothing* from their lesson last night? They'd been supremely lucky he hadn't sent them both straight to hell!

By his grace, and his grace alone, they'd been given a chance to redeem themselves. To repent of their sinful ways. It had been a novel sensation, knowing he'd given someone forgiveness, had granted them life. But to throw his reprieve in his face like this!

Oh, they would surely die now.

They would bleed until their sins were purged, would bathe in their own blood until they were washed clean. And then they would *die.* Both of them. He'd make sure of it next time.

And now he knew where they were staying. How very convenient that they'd wandered right onto his home turf like this. Hapless little flies. Didn't even know they'd just landed in the spider's web.

Oh, but they would. They would.

Chapter 7

Maddie frowned as they made their way back to the resort proper. She heard the faint, but distinct sounds of Donna Summer's music. What was the classic disco queen doing belting out a tune in a place like this?

Tom's arm tightened across her shoulder. "Everything okay?" he murmured, his head turned toward her, but his eyes roving everywhere but on her.

"Yes. Why do you ask?"

"You frowned."

"How would you know that? You weren't looking at me," she replied.

"I felt it."

"How?"

"I'm psychic."

"Seriously?"

He stopped in the middle of the path. Fully faced her.

"Actually, I kind of am. If you work in a business like mine for long enough, you develop a sixth sense about stuff. Mind you, I don't rely solely on gut feeling to do my job, but I do pay attention to it." He grinned boyishly at her. "Besides, you hunch up your shoulders a little whenever you frown. I felt the hunch."

Okay, he got full points for noticing details. But part of her was disappointed that it wasn't some sort of romantic simpatico between them that made him aware of her frown. "When did Donna Summer fly into Vanua Taru?"

He looked perplexed for a moment, then grinned. "Ah. The music. Paradise Cove has a hot disco. When there's not a cyclone bearing down on the place, people cruise in on yachts from other islands and even fly in for the evening to party there. There are usually live bands. The joint's always crammed. But I expect they're spinning vinyls tonight."

"People still use vinyl records?"

He shrugged. "Nigel says when the only thing you need is loud noise and a beat, a record does the job just as well as modern technology…and they have higher 'cool factor.'"

She smiled. "Well, if Nigel says records are cool, I guess they are."

Tom turned and continued up the path, still holding her hand.

"How long have you been in the bodyguard business, Tom?"

"'Bout eight hours."

She rolled her eyes. "Before you came to Vanua Taru?"

"Nearly twenty years."

"Let's see. That would make you about sixty-eight years old."

"Hey! Enough wisecracks about me being an old man. I'm forty-one."

Dang. He was sure well preserved for forty-one. She'd have placed him in his mid-thirties if she had to guess. His body was lean and hard, his thick, dark hair showing not even a hint of gray. He didn't even have laugh lines at the corner of his eyes to speak of.

"What do you do to stay looking so young?"

He laughed helplessly. "I give up. Pardon me while I kick up my heels and die of old age."

She clarified hastily. "I didn't mean it like that. I meant it as a compliment. You look…great." Her breath hitched a little as she stopped to consider just how great he did look tonight. She didn't even care that he was violently underdressed or that a shadow of danger darkened his eyes. She just wanted to grab his shirt, pull him close and take the kiss she could already taste. The kiss she craved.

He'd shaved before supper and his cheeks were smooth and tanned. Her fingertips itched to caress his face. To drift lower, tracing the muscular column of his neck, the hollow of his collarbone, to his muscle-slabbed ribs, his abdomen, which she knew would go rock hard beneath her touch. She distinctly recalled the thin line of dark hair that led downward from his navel, pointing the way to hidden treasures lower down. Mmm. To trace that path with her lips. To lick him like an ice-cream cone…

"You can stop that now."

His voice rasped harshly against her ears.

She blinked, startled out of her reverie. "Stop what?"

"Looking at me as if I'm an edible treat."

Her lips curved up. She didn't even have to say the words aloud. She just leaned forward slowly. First, her breasts, all but pulsing with need, rubbed against his shirt. She groaned in pleasure.

He groaned in pain.

Then she took a small step closer, and her thigh nestled between his. Her hip felt the hard length of him growing harder by the second. She purred her delight.

He growled his discomfort.

She looped her arms around his neck, toying with the soft hair at the back of his neck. And then she stood on tiptoe and licked his lips. Sipped at him, really, savoring the fullness of his lower lip, the way his mouth opened for her, the smooth slide of her tongue across the edge of his teeth.

It was back. All of it. The thundering lust, the pounding need, the uncontrollable wildness that begged her to rip his shirt off, push him to the ground and make love to him right here on the path. To ride him until he shouted his pleasure into the night.

She begged him to do just that.

He swore violently…and refused.

"I'm working," he explained desperately. "I have to keep my wits about me. Protect you from this bastard. I can't…you're too…dammit, I can't think about anything else when I make love to you!"

She pouted.

He apologized. "Honey, that was a compliment. You blow me away. We're…incredible together…it's a *good* thing that I can't think when you kiss me like that…"

She pouted some more.

"Aww, hell."

He kissed her back.

Tom didn't know how long they stood in the middle of the path and tried to inhale each other's lungs, but he did know his knees had gone weak and most of the blood in his body had pooled far, far away from his brain before he finally tore himself away from her.

Maddie was warm and sinuous in his arms, as sleek as a mink. He reached for the hem of her dress, lifting it so he could grasp her buttocks, firm and juicy in his hand. A low moan slipped from her throat…oh, yeah. Right here. Right now. On the beach.

Wait…Sex on the Beach…Killer…

He came up for air, swearing violently.

She dropped her forehead to his chest, panting. At least he wasn't the only one struggling for control. They staggered up the long flights of steps, lost in the lust clutching them both in its grip. So *this* was how the Sex on the Beach Killer was able to sneak up on his victims and stab them to death. If the guy had been standing behind them a moment ago, he'd have been completely helpless to defend himself or Maddie. Hell, he was barely able to form rational thoughts now.

The disco was loud and crowded when they entered. A hurricane party was in full swing, and most of the Cove's guests were drinking and dancing with abandon. Beside him, Maddie assessed the room with the practiced eye of an experienced party girl. She moved unerringly toward a cluster of "beautiful people" in the far corner. He didn't know the faces she'd targeted, but he definitely knew the type. Rich, debauched and wild.

Yup, she had a good instinct for the money in a room. The young men in the group looked jaded, bored by the cover models draped all over their laps. Although in the guys' defense, the models looked just as bored. He recalled well the vapid expressions, the inability to answer simple questions, to follow basic logic. Whether they just weren't that sharp, or their brains were so fried from the drugs they consumed like candy was hard to tell.

How could Maddie stand to be around people like that? She was so bright and clever, how could she even talk to them? Interested, he tagged along to see how she fared. Soon enough, it became clear. She focused her conversational efforts on those in the group who had a few functional brain cells left and ignored the others, who were well on their way to wasted, their eyes bloodshot, their speech slurred. As a group, they smelled bad, looked sloppy and were completely unattractive in every way.

Good Lord. Had he looked like that when he'd gone on his benders over the past few months? The thought disgusted him. Why had it suddenly occurred to him to wonder about that, of all things? Of course, he only had to look up to see the answer. Maddie's sparkling laughter twinkled right through him, and the intelligence in her gaze was balm to his soul.

As he gazed at her, one of the drunks made a clumsy pass at Maddie. Tom surged forward to swat the guy's paws off her, but before he got there, Maddie smoothly captured the guy's roaming hands and unobtrusively replaced them in the kid's own lap. No fuss, no muss, nobody embarrassed. *Nicely done. Classy.*

Tom subsided as she glanced up, made eye contact with him and smiled self-deprecatingly. Why would a hardcore party girl, like Maddie portrayed herself to be, make the effort to save a drunk she'd likely never see again from a little humiliation? In his experience, the women prowling these clubs were looking for sex, drugs and rich boyfriends. They didn't do things like she just had. Yet again, her outward physical persona jarred with her actions. He frowned, perplexed.

One of the less drunk guys asked Maddie to dance, and she glanced over at Tom for permission. He gestured for her to go ahead. It would give him a chance to scope out the room and see if any six-foot-tall, athletic, Caucasian males showed an unusual interest in her.

A hard-driving dance tune blared from the speakers, and Maddie broke into a well-choreographed series of dance combinations. She looked like a cheerleader for a professional sports team. It was slick, practiced and easy on the eye. But the artifice of it left him cold. He leaned back in the booth and casually checked out the room's occupants. Most everyone was involved in shaking their booty or dumping alcoholic libations down the hatch. Maddie's dancing drew a fair bit of attention, nothing beyond ordinary interest, though.

But then, on the far side of the room, in the deeply shadowed alcove of an employee doorway, a faint movement caught Tom's eye. A tall, trim figure lurked deep in the shadows. The man's gaze methodically swept the room, scoping it out as intently and thoroughly as Tom was doing. The guy's gaze lighted on Maddie, slid on. Stopped. Came back to her. Narrowed.

Tom half rose out of his seat. Bingo.

But then the man moved forward a step. Tom laughed under his breath, and sank back into the seat in relief. Just Nigel. Of course he checked out the room like a pro. He *was* a pro.

The song ended and Maddie came back to the table, collapsing into the booth beside him, laughing. One of the only semidrunk guys made an inane comment about how maybe she could give him a private show later.

Maddie made an appropriately vague reply and slid closer to Tom, smiling up at him flirtatiously. "Did you like my dancing, too?"

He shrugged. "Yeah. Sure. As mating dances go, it wasn't half bad. Most of the men in the room watched you."

"Mating! You didn't like it," she accused.

"You performed just fine. I'm curious, though. Do you ever dance just for the fun of it?"

She turned a perplexed look on him. "I spent a solid year learning how to dance like that." When he cocked a skeptical eyebrow, she added faintly defensively, "Dance class was fun. Really."

He nodded, smiling gently. "Right."

"I suppose you can do better on a dance floor?" she challenged.

He shrugged. "Nah. But I have fun when I do it. Dancing's about feeling the music and the moment. I'm not into prefabbed routines designed to attract a rich boyfriend."

She looked distinctly stung, and opened her mouth to retort. He was surprised when she stood up instead. "Fine, twinkletoes. Let's see what you've got."

He grinned and slid out of the booth. They had to walk past the DJ's booth on their way to the floor, and he stopped to murmur in the fellow's ear. Tom had helped the guy, a local, a few months back with a belligerent ex-brother-in-law, and the DJ owed him one. He grinned and nodded at Tom's request.

Tom rested his hand in the small of Maddie's back. Her sharp, indrawn breath stoked the slow burn of desire that seemed to be his constant companion around her. The current song ended, and a new one began.

Her eyebrows shot up, and he grinned at her chagrin. It was a slow, sexy, saxophone piece that wailed as smooth as melted chocolate, seducing couples onto the floor. Tom drew her into his arms. Holding her this way felt like coming home. Funny, how in all the months of binge drinking he'd never truly become addicted to alcohol. But after one day with this woman, she was a fire in his blood that he couldn't possibly get enough of.

She moved faintly awkwardly in his arms, as if she wanted to do something but was holding back.

"Relax," he murmured against her temple. "Feel the music. Just let yourself move to it."

She grumbled, "That's not the problem."

He drew back enough to gaze down at her in the dim light. Her eyelashes were long and dark as she peeked up at him through them. "Okay, I'll bite. What's wrong?"

"I want to crawl inside your shirt and feel your skin. I want to nibble your ear and hear that groan you make in the back of your throat. I want…I want you inside me, moving to the music and filling me up."

"Oh, jeez."

She smiled ruefully. "Yeah. That groan."

"Next time, we'll have music."

"What about the beach? I thought we're supposed to do it in public, or at least pretend to, and try to draw out you-know-who."

"That's business. I'm talking about the next time we're alone. In private. Where we don't have to worry about anything but making love until neither of us can stand."

She laid her head on his shoulder. "Mmm. I like the sound of that."

She was pure heaven in his arms, unabashedly plastered against him from neck to knee, boneless and mellow, swaying easily in his arms. Okay, so she could seriously dance. It made him imagine her melting all over him like this when they were horizontal. Of their bodies fusing into one, formless and weightless, floating along on a river of music, sometimes rushing toward oblivion, sometimes pounding hard on rocks of sound, sometimes gliding along so smooth and easy that flesh could barely feel its caress.

Once the image lodged in his brain, nothing and no one was going to remove it.

Lost in a delicious agony of need, he led her off the floor when the song ended. In unspoken, mutual agreement, they moved toward the exit, their arms entwined around each other's waists. Maddie gazed up at him with naked desire, and he indulged in staring deep into her smoky eyes. It was a rare event when he let his real feelings show, particularly in public. But with Maddie, it was so damned easy. He fell into playing her besotted lover as naturally as breathing.

Except…this was work. He had to maintain—and contain—the driving lust surging through his gut *and* keep his brain engaged. Dammit, didn't Sheriff Marquez understand that men weren't wired that way? There was only blood enough in his body to keep one major organ functioning at full capacity. And at the moment, it damned well wasn't his brain!

The recipe for catching the killer was simple. Use himself and Maddie as bait. Fan the incendiary attraction between them into a public wildfire, then adjourn to the beach to wait for the murderer to strike.

Of course, this whole business of falling for the girl wasn't part of that plan. When they were alone together, he could so easily lose himself in her, go crazy for her and start thinking about things like spending the rest of his life with her. Thankfully the public, Madeline C. persona she showed the world was off-putting enough to him that he was managing to hang on to a thread of sanity…a thin one, but a thread, nonetheless.

Grasping at that fragile thread, he tucked Maddie's hand

under his elbow and headed for the beachside door. It was no great feat of acting to pass through the crowd as if it weren't there, so involved were they in one another. He didn't look at anyone else, didn't block out a path for her, didn't use his body to protect her from possible sight lines a shooter might use. It went contrary to everything he'd ever been taught about protecting a client. But it was the only way to draw the attention of the Sex on the Beach Killer. The guy was too smart to fall for a blatant trap. He and Maddie had to, no kidding, be so wrapped up in one another they couldn't see straight. Thankfully, that wasn't a stretch for either of them.

The very cursory glance he'd had time to take at the killer's file indicated that the fellow could sniff two things like a bloodhound. Cops and sex. Which is probably why Marquez was so hot and bothered to force a non-cop onto the case. As a private operator, he might not trigger the killer's cop-warning system.

Not to mention that the scent of sex hung over him and Maddie as thickly as the pall of smoke hovering in the club. All the two of them had to do was be in the same room, and sexual vibes rippled off them like heat waves in the desert sun. Without exception, the killer went after couples reported to have been crawling all over each other and all but having sex in front of audiences shortly before their murders. When the lovers eventually adjourned to the beach, the killer moved in on them.

He held the door for Maddie and she slipped by him, blatantly brushing against him on her way past. Vixen. As if he wasn't already turned on enough. He smiled down at her, silently promising sweet revenge.

Her eyes snapped in eager anticipation.

He guided her across the wide porch and down the stairs to

the beach. The spot exactly between his shoulder blades itched ferociously all of a sudden. Excellent. He only got that horrible feeling of having a target on his back when someone was studying him intently. *C'mon, you slimy bastard. Take the bait.*

They hadn't quite dropped out of sight of the disco's picture windows when he paused, pulling Maddie into his arms, attempting to extract her tonsils with his tongue.

Oh, man. She tasted like raspberries and mustard. Rich and creamy. Melting across his tongue and filling his head with her effervescence. With him standing one step below her, it put their bodies into perfect belly-to-belly alignment.

She flung herself against him, groaning her need. "What are you doing to me? I never lust after guys like this."

"Haven't you figured it out yet? I'm not just any guy, honey." He propped one foot on the step she stood on. She rubbed high against his inner thigh, and then higher, drawing a groan of his own out of him.

He speared one hand into her hair, holding her in place so his mouth could plunder hers. He drank deeply of her, his head spinning with the taste and smell of her desire.

She tore her mouth away, gasping. "I'm going to faint if you keep that up."

He laughed low, almost a growl. "Those punks back in the disco are boys. They don't know how to pleasure a woman. They're only thinking about getting their own rocks off. When I'm done with you, fainting will be the least of your worries."

He leaned down enough to hook his fingers around the back of her knee. He drew her thigh up and over his bent one, looping it around his hips. His fingers slid up the back of her sleek leg, approaching her feminine flesh and feeling the heat of her growing and growing.

Her hips rolled forward, seeking his touch, seeking the

release already building within her. He could feel it in the vibrations emanating from low in her belly and radiating outward.

His fingers slid across her bare buttocks. Had she gone commando? The thought of her sitting through that formal dinner in that fancy restaurant wearing no underwear made him want to throw her down right here and pound into her until they both fainted.

She arched her whole body forward now, offering up her breasts to him. Her erect nipples strained against the thin silk. He leaned down and captured one in his mouth through the flimsy fabric. He bit down just hard enough to wring a cry of pleasure-pain from her.

She writhed on his thigh, her nether parts chafing against his in desperate supplication. His fingers slid farther forward and touched her throbbing, wet heat.

A thong. She was wearing a thong. The thought just about sent him over the edge. He slipped the tip of his finger beneath the fabric barrier and just inside her tight opening. She flowed around him, as warm and sweet and pulsing as he remembered. His own flesh throbbed in time with hers, grating against his clothes painfully.

Her fingers slipped between them, measuring the length of him behind his zipper. He was rock hard, and even that fleeting touch was enough to make him exhale hard on an impulse to rip her clothes off.

Nuzzling her chest, he discovered that the soft drape of her neckline had enough slack in it that he could pull it to one side and get his mouth on naked skin. He drew her breast into his mouth and rolled around the cherry of her nipple with his tongue, sucking at it and grazing it with his teeth in chaotic abandon.

His zipper slid down, rattling against his shaft as the teeth vibrated loose one by one. He about jumped out of his skin.

Beach. They had to get down to the beach. He couldn't for the life of him remember why. But he was going to lay her down on the sand, spread her wide open and ride her until she couldn't remember her name.

He took a step back. Another. Whimpering, she followed him, chasing him with hands and mouth and body. How they made it down the long staircase to the beach, he had no real recollection. But somewhere on the way down, she released him from his pants and used his length as a handle, running the pad of her thumb across his slick tip until he nearly exploded.

And then the uneven softness of sand made him stumble. Oh, God. Yes. They'd made it. He grasped her buttocks in both hands and lifted her up. She wrapped her legs and arms around him, devouring his mouth in rhythm to the rocking of her hips against him.

Frantic, he searched around for a spot secluded enough that they wouldn't be interrupted. Where he would see anyone approaching…if he could actually see at all. In another few seconds, his eyeballs were going to explode along with the rest of him. He was a volcano about to blow.

He fell to his knees. Leaned over, dumping Maddie onto her back. He tore off that maddening thong in a single violent movement, flinging it aside.

"Yes. Yes. Now, now," she chanted, breathless.

He rocked back on his knees, burying his face between her legs, inhaling the scent of her, dragging his tongue up the length of her pulsing flesh from her opening to the swollen nub of her desire. Her thighs trembled beneath his hands and she gave a sharp cry. He licked again, and another keening cry tore from her throat. She thrashed beneath him, surging up, reaching for him with both hands.

He pinned her arms against the sand and she fought,

mindless, wild with need. He kneed her thighs open. And slammed home his rock-hard flesh all the way to the hilt. The very center of her pushed against him, and her female muscles convulsed around him, drenching him in liquid heat.

He supported his upper body nearly upright, his knees digging deep into the sand, both to give him the right angle and an unobstructed view of the beach. He partially withdrew and slid home again. Hard. Maddie no longer formed words beneath him, singing her lust in moans and shuddering cries and ragged breaths. She bucked up against his hands again where they held her arms down and a note of surprise crept into her shout of release.

A grin of male satisfaction curved his mouth. And if she thought that was great…

He drove into her over and over, churning with the force of a piston, his entire body vibrating with each stroke as he buried himself to the hilt, stretching her to the very limit to take all of him. The ocean roared behind them, primal. Wild. Violent.

She screamed her pleasure.

"Sing for me, baby," he groaned.

She screamed again. More and even more heat drenched him, scorching him, slick and so wet.

Oh, yeah. He picked up the pace, his buttocks clenching tighter and tighter as his own climax built to towering proportions. His breath hitched. Held. Her entire body quivered around him, poised on the edge of an epic orgasm. And he delivered the coup de grâce—a final stroke that touched her very core. His back arched like a bow, and his entire body clenched. And then the world exploded. Stars burst before his eyes, and his orgasm ripped all the way out to his fingertips and toes. Damned if his hair didn't feel like it had caught on fire.

He'd have collapsed on top of her were his elbows not locked, and some subliminal need to stay marginally upright keeping him from going completely boneless.

Something thudded softly into the sand not far from them. He lurched, startled. Not that being startled in any way equated to his brain commencing normal functioning, however. It was just a rock. Fist-size. Loose scree from the cliff above. Another rock tumbled past, clicking against the cliff face before half burying itself in the sand. Damn. They were bringing the cliff down around them.

He swore under his breath, as much in awe as in shock at what they'd just done. He never was that…raw…with a woman, never gave in to unleashed desire like that. Never gave over every last ounce of his being to another human being.

"Are you okay?" he managed to gasp.

A shaky laugh and another shudder that passed through her entire body was his only answer.

He'd take that as a yes.

Sand showered down from above. A small sliver of sanity returned to him. Enough to take a quick, surreptitious glance around the beach. No one. He glanced up. About forty feet up, it looked like a ledge protruded slightly. From here, he couldn't see the shelf. But anyone peering down over the edge of it would've had an unobstructed view of them. His skin crawled with sudden certainty. The killer had been up there just now. And just as certainly, the falling rocks and sand were the remnants of the guy's departure.

If the killer had been up there, he'd gotten a hell of a show. Surprising that he hadn't struck. Tom studied the cliff more closely. Fortunately, to get down to the beach from that ledge, the guy would've had to climb back up the cliff face and come down the stairs. And those were far too exposed for the guy to have made a stealthy approach to them.

Although, he and Maddie had been so caught up in what they were doing, the killer could have walked up to them and asked the time of day and neither of them would have noticed.

Icy fear raced through him at that realization. They'd been as vulnerable as any of the dead couples. *He'd failed to protect Maddie.* Had the killer struck a few moments ago, the two of them would be *dead.* Self-recrimination shredded his gut to ribbons. He was weak. Washed up. Incapable of doing what Marquez had asked of him. He swore long and violently to himself.

What kind of *moron* had a vicious serial killer chasing him and stopped to have sex in the midst of evading the killer?

Him, apparently. If there were an anatomically possible way to kick himself hard in the butt, he'd do it right now. He'd been dumb, dumb, dumb!

The first order of business was to get Maddie off this beach and park her somewhere safe. Then he had to get in touch with Marquez and let the guy know that alternate protection for her had to be arranged immediately, cyclone or no cyclone.

Maddie moved restlessly beneath him. He helped her sit up and attempted to no avail to brush the sand off her wadded clothes and out of her hair.

She shook her head and sand flew every which way. "I need a shower," she laughed.

"That can be arranged." He helped her to her feet and retrieved her strappy little thong and strappy little shoes for her. They readjusted their clothing and started down the beach. She made a turn for the stairs they'd come down, and Tom restrained her gently.

"Let's take the other set of stairs closer to our villa."

"You don't want to be seen in the disco looking like you just got lucky?" she asked curiously. "Most guys want to flaunt the fact that they just got some."

He wrinkled his nose in distaste. "I'd like to think I have more tact than that. I don't care if anyone knows I got the girl or not. I'd just rather be alone with you. And this ocean is incredible."

She glanced over her shoulder at the massive breakers rolling ashore. He did the same. Wave crests crashed down, demolishing the water beneath and sending up huge spumes of spray. "How much worse will this get?"

"I dunno. I've never seen a major cyclone up close and personal. I hear the storm surge is the most destructive part—more so than the wind."

"How tall are these cliffs, again?" she asked in alarm.

"At least fifty feet. Kato's storm surge is forecasted to be around seventeen feet."

"I like that math," she replied, sounding relieved.

While the giant breakers distracted her, Tom pulled out his cell phone and dialed the sheriff's phone number. A few months back, he'd programmed the phone number of every permanent resident on the island into his cell phone out of sheer boredom during an early attempt to climb out of the bottle.

"Yeah?" Marquez growled after several rings.

"It's Tom Laruso. I can't do it. I can't protect Maddie. You've got to come get her. We're at Paradise Cove."

"What the hell am I supposed to do with her, Laruso? In case you haven't noticed, I've got a cyclone bearing down on my island."

Tom sighed. "I don't care. Keep her with you." At Marquez's snort of not-a-chance-in-hell, Tom added, "Lock her up in jail, then. But I can't do this. I've lost the edge. I'm making basic mistakes."

"Yeah, but at least you know they're basic mistakes. Not one of my guys has any personal-protection training. And I don't have time for her. I haven't slept in two days, and I'm not going to get much more than quick naps for the next week. You're gonna have to handle Miss Crummby yourself."

That was the problem, dammit. He was handling her far too much!

"But—"

"No buts, Laruso. You're the best we've got for the job. Suck it up and deal with it, or else I'll deputize you and order you to do it anyway." Marquez disconnected.

Sonofa— Tom pocketed the phone and swore some more under his breath. He couldn't do this! But it looked as if he had to give it a go, anyway.

Thing was, this wasn't just about him being an idiot and getting distracted by sex. It was about fear. Abject, gut-churning, knee-knocking fear that something bad would happen to Maddie on his watch. He cared about her, dammit! He was way too close to her emotionally to be an effective bodyguard. Maybe he should ask Nigel to take over. Except Nigel didn't have personal-protection training either, and the guy had his hands more than full battening down the hatches to ride out the storm and taking care of several hundred guests of the resort.

He was stuck with the job, no matter how badly he did it. No matter that he wasn't fit to do it. No matter that Maddie's life hung in the balance.

He was going to puke now.

Maddie stopped beside him, and Tom realized they'd arrived at the narrow stone staircase which wound up the cliff not far from their villa. Basic-security technique dictated that he go up first, even though he'd have enjoyed following her and partaking of the view of her pert backside. He had to stop having thoughts like that! Yeah, right. He could stop breathing on command, too.

They arrived at the top of the cliff and he turned right, heading down the path toward their villa. The ocean noise didn't drown out all the jungle sounds up here. Insects buzzed and clicked and chirped. The night air was warmer, too. Sticky on his skin. Heavy and oppressive. Made for sweaty sex and lazy ceiling fans.

The dark bulk of their villa came into view. He fumbled with the plastic key card, and Maddie giggled as she tried to help him jam it in the lock. Between the two of them, they managed to gain entrance to the *bure*.

Just inside the door, she turned into his arms, kissing him with mouth and hands and body, stripping him out of his shirt as they twirled toward the bathroom and a hot, naked shower. Their clothes pinwheeled away from them as they made their way across the living room.

He unzipped her dress and she stepped out of it. It pooled on the floor, and she took a moment to scoop it up, laughing. "This cost you a fortune. I'd hate to ruin it. Let me toss it on a hanger."

He took the opportunity to enjoy the swanlike line of her naked back rising from the sexiest black thong he'd ever seen. They'd been lucky to find it on the beach in the dark after he'd flung it away in such haste. She pulled a hanger out of the closet and he reached for the zipper of his shorts. Damned if he didn't want her again, already.

"My shoes." Something broke in her voice. Dawning realization. *Fear.*

"Your shoes?" Warning alarms exploded in his brain, but he struggled to form logical thought past his raging hormones.

"What's wrong with your shoes?" He stumbled over to the closet and looked over her shoulder. They were lined up neatly in a row. Just like she'd left them, right?

"They've been moved. The espadrilles don't go with that outfit. The cork sandals do. The espadrilles should be lined up under the sundress."

Belatedly, his protective instincts broke through the lust, and he grabbed her, wrapping her in a protective embrace that had nothing to do with sex. Cripes. He hadn't even cleared the place when they came in. He had no idea where to put her that was safe. An intruder could be in the back of the closet, the bathroom. Hell, under the bed. For lack of anyplace else to secure her, he poked his head into the closet fast. It checked out empty, and he shoved her inside. "Stay down," he bit out tersely.

She stared up at him, wide-eyed in terror, as he pulled his gun out of the holster tucked in the back of his shorts and growled, "I'll be back in a minute. Don't move."

She nodded and he leaped away, throwing open the bathroom door and spinning into the space low and fast. *Clear.* Under the bed. *Clear.* Behind the breakfast bar. *Clear.* One by one, he checked every possible hiding space in the villa that could conceal a human being. He pulled down the shades and closed the curtains while he was at it, all the while berating himself. Sloppy, sloppy, sloppy. He clicked off the lights. No need to cast any shadows for the killer to watch from outside the *bure.*

Maddie squeaked when the place went dark.

"It's okay, honey. I turned off the lights. It's all clear. I'm coming to get you." When he slid the door open, she tumbled out of the closet and into his arms, shaking in terror.

"Why is this happening to us?" she quavered against his chest.

"Why does it happen to anyone? We were in the wrong place at the wrong time." Is that what had happened to Arielle? Had she crossed paths with the wrong weirdo at the wrong time? Someone who knew her or knew of her, and took the opportunity to murder a famous pop star and gain immortality?

"What do we do now?" Maddie whispered.

"Now, I make a couple of phone calls, while you stay plastered to my side."

"I like that plan."

He guided her over to the bed and sat on the edge of it. He pulled her down into his lap, reached over for the telephone and punched the button for housekeeping.

"Hi, this is the Clifftop Villa. Did any of your people come out here to straighten up while we were at dinner?"

"No, sir," a polite voice said on the other end of the line.

"No turndown service?"

"No, sir. My records show you having requested that we call you and obtain permission before we send anyone into your villa for any reason. Is that incorrect?"

"No. That's exactly right. I was just checking. Thanks." Tom hung up the phone, thinking fast. He punched another button, this time the hotel operator. "I need you to get Nigel Cumberland on the horn. Now. Yes, it's an emergency. I'll wait."

That appropriately alarmed the operator, and she agreed to track down the manager immediately.

Were it not for Maddie on his lap, he'd be pacing like a caged tiger. Along with feelings of inadequacy as a bodyguard, now guilt roared through him, too. He *knew* better than to fool around on the job. And he sure as *hell* knew not to have sex with the client—on duty or off. The Sex on the Beach Killer was close by, waiting to strike, to *kill* them, for God's sake! He deserved to die for his stupidity. Problem was, if he went, Maddie went, too. And she emphatically didn't deserve to die. He swore violently under his breath. Like it or not, there would be no more fooling around between them until the bastard was caught.

While he waited for the Brit to come to the phone, he ordered Maddie tersely, "Get dressed and pack your things. We're getting out of here."

"Can I turn on a light?"

"You can turn on the bathroom lights. And you can crack the bathroom door open if you need a little light in here to see by. Be quick, sweetheart. Don't worry about being neat."

She dropped a brief kiss on his neck and moved away to do as he instructed. He watched her move around the dark room, reaching into the closet for clothes. She pulled out the white sundress.

"Not white. Wear something dark," he instructed quietly.

She gulped and nodded, and hastily put the sundress back. He watched her pull on dark shorts and a tank top, bending and straightening, sliding fabric up her long, slim legs, smoothing cotton down over her womanly curves. Man, she was a looker.

"Cumberland, here."

Tom replied tightly, "We've had an intruder at our villa. I need a ride out of here. Now."

"How soon can you be ready to go?" Nigel asked.

"Five minutes ago."

"Roger. Two minutes. Shoreside."

"Thanks. And Nigel? Come with your lights off."

"Off?" The former policeman sounded startled for a moment, but then responded calmly. "Got it. Will do."

Tom hung up the phone and pulled his duffel bag out from under the bed. He zipped it quickly. There. Packed. Old habit—never unpack, for just this reason. Two seconds, and he was ready to roll.

"Need any help?" he asked Maddie.

"Almost done," she called from the bathroom.

"You've got a minute and thirty seconds."

She skidded to the front door with her last bag in hand ten seconds before her allotted time ran out.

"Not bad for a woman," he commented, grinning, as he eased the shoreside door open and took a hard look around.

She stuck her tongue out at him. "I've no doubt ruined at least half of my new clothes."

He snorted. "Live through this and I'll buy you more."

Her gaze narrowed. "I'll hold you to that. Great clothes are serious business, I'll have you know."

He opened his mouth to make a droll retort but was drowned out by the crunch of tires on gravel. The quiet rumble of an engine announced that their ride was not one of the ubiquitous golf carts so prevalent on the island. It turned out to be a white pickup truck sporting the Paradise Cove logo on its door.

Tom and Nigel traded nods as the former opened the passenger-side door and deposited Maddie inside, instructing her to lie down across the seat. Tom eased the door shut and leaped lightly into the bed of the pickup truck, crouching with his back against the cab, scanning all around. Damn, it was dark out here. Good weather conditions for an escape. Better conditions for a kill.

He banged the roof of the cab lightly. The vehicle moved out.

Chapter 8

Maddie all but fell to the floor as the truck lurched into motion, her head practically in Nigel's lap. He stiffened instantly.

"Sorry," she mumbled up at him, embarrassed. His jaw clenched rock hard. He glanced down at her and the look in his eye was so intent she'd almost call it ferocious. But then, unaccountably, he grinned. "Having fun yet?"

"I have to admit," she replied ruefully, "this business of being a damsel in distress isn't all it's cracked up to be."

He patted the dashboard. "How do you like my white charger?"

"It's perfect."

"Which is to say it's running?" he retorted dryly.

"Exactly."

As her eyes adjusted to the dark, she frowned at the underside of the dashboard. What was that thing sticking out under there? It didn't look like any truck part she'd ever seen before.

And growing up on a farm, she was plenty familiar with the interiors of pickup trucks. She stared at the protrusion as her night vision continued to come in. Slowly, the hilt of a knife took shape, sticking out of a sheath that was attached to the underside of the dashboard by some invisible means. Apprehension blossomed in her gut. Holy cow. That looked like a big knife—almost machetelike in proportions. Of course, living on a tropical island like this, a sticker like that probably came in handy. Did Tom have a knife like that?

Startled that it had taken this long for it to occur to her, she blurted, "Where's Tom?" She started to sit up to look for him, but Nigel put a big hand on her shoulder and gently kept her down.

"He's in the back with a gun, acting as our spotter."

"I don't know what that is, but it sounds impressive," she replied.

The truck turned off the rough gravel and accelerated down a paved road. After about two minutes, Nigel reached up and slid open the small rear window. "Where to?" he called.

"My place."

Nigel nodded and then murmured, "You can sit up now."

Maddie was happy to comply. She'd been starting to get a little carsick, lying on her side in the dark, staring at Nigel's knife.

She looked around, noting the blackness all around them. "Good grief!" she exclaimed. "How can you see a thing?"

He shrugged. "I have pretty good eyesight." The truck rounded a bend in the sandy track and Tom's *bure* loomed in the darkness. Even over the sound of the engine, she heard surf pounding nearby.

Tom said through the window, "Let me clear the house, first. Then I'll be back for you."

She nodded as he jumped out of the truck and disappeared. Suddenly, she felt very alone in this small space with a man she barely knew. The jungle pressing in around them felt forbidding. Menacing, even. This whole Sex on the Beach Killer thing was really messing with her head. What if Tom didn't come back? Raw panic speared into her at the thought.

But on the heels of her panic came the sure and certain knowledge that Tom would come back to her, hell or high water. He was just that kind of man. He would never abandon her. He had promised to keep her safe and he'd die if necessary to keep that promise. He was the kind of man a girl could trust…forever.

She stared out into the night, stunned at the thought. She was *not* attaching the word forever to anything that had to do with her and Tom Laruso!

Was she?

Madeline C., she thought weakly. Her plan…a rich husband who'd take care of her…

And in that moment, knowing exploded in her consciousness. There were different kinds of security, and money was only one of them. The kind of security Tom offered was another…perhaps even more powerful…kind of security. The kind that never wavered for richer, for poorer, in sickness and in health…

Oh, crap.

She'd done a bad thing. A very, very bad thing. She'd fallen for Tom Laruso.

In a minute or two, Tom materialized out of nowhere by her truck window, and she jumped a mile high. How did he do that? She'd been looking for him and still hadn't seen him coming. He opened the door for her and held out his hand. She laid her icy hand in his warm one and his fingers closed around hers, comfortably. Reassuringly. Yup. The kind of guy a girl could trust with her life. All of it, from now till death did they part.

Shivers tore through her from head to foot.

"Let's go, sweetheart," he murmured. "Once you're safely under cover, I'll come back for your bags."

She glanced back over her shoulder as he whisked her into the night. "Thanks, Nigel."

"No worries," the Brit called back to her.

Tom ushered her into his *bure,* his bulk hovering close enough to chase away the boogeyman. His body warmth reached out to her, almost a caress in the cavernous dark. The night and the villa wrapped around them as thick and heavy as a familiar wool blanket. *Safe.* She let out a long breath of relief.

Tom's disembodied voice floated from nearby. "I'm going to booby-trap the doors and windows. So don't touch any of them, okay?"

"Booby-trap? As in blowing up?"

"Nothing quite that violent. I'm just attaching noisemakers to all of them. If someone tries to break and enter, alarms will go off and make a ton of noise."

"What kind of alarms?"

"I'll attach motion-activated sensors to both doors. And I've got firecrackers I'll rig to trip wires in front of the big windows. The kitchen window will get a high-tech pile of delicately balanced pots and pans."

She grinned her appreciation of that one. Her parents had caught her sneaking in late after missing a curfew one night in high school, using the exact same technique. She knew from experience that it was highly effective.

As a gust howled past the villa, she asked dubiously, "All this wind won't rattle one of your alarms into going off?"

Now that she wasn't living in mortal fear of being shot any second, she registered that the wind was noticeably stronger than it had been even an hour ago.

"By the time the wind's blowing hard enough to set off my alarms, nobody will be out running around, anyway. Even our killer will have to take cover."

"Could you call him something besides 'our killer'? That phrase gives me the willies. It sounds entirely too prophetic for my taste."

Tom laughed. "Sure. How about the resident Vanua Taru sicko?"

"Not much better, but better," she replied wryly. "How much longer until the cyclone gets here, anyway?"

"The outer rain bands have already arrived. From here on out, the weather will just get worse. The eye wall is due to hit around midmorning tomorrow."

"And this thatched roof will be okay in high winds?"

"Yup. I secured boards over it to help hold it down yesterday before I flew over to the big island to pick you up. Woven thatch is pretty durable stuff, according to the locals. As long as the wind doesn't lift it up and peel it back—hence the boards—it'll stand up to anything Kato can throw at it. I'm told these cantilevered log structures flex well in the face of a storm and don't tear apart."

"What about your windows?"

"While you were shopping today, I came back here and screwed all of the storm shutters closed."

"Really? Who'd have guessed you were so prepared? You're a regular boy scout!"

He snorted. "You don't have to sound *that* surprised."

"Do we still have water and power?"

"Water, yes. This place has an underground cistern that

collects rainwater. I have a hand pump we can use to draw up water from it. As for electricity, not for much longer, if I had to guess. Sheriff Marquez will shut down the island's main generator as soon as he thinks the power lines are in danger of being blown down. Live wires in the streets are bad things. I wouldn't be surprised if he's already pulled the plug. But I don't want us to turn on any lights, regardless. No candles, either. Nothing to signal to anybody that we're here."

"By anybody, you mean the Sex on the Beach Killer," she retorted.

"Precisely."

She asked lightly, "What *are* we going to do in the dark to pass the time with no power and no lamps or candles?" Anticipation fluttered through her at the thought of taking that shower she'd started with Tom over at the other *bure*.

His regretful sigh floated out of the dark. "We can't."

She didn't even have to ask what he was talking about. Or why. *His job.* He took his bodyguarding duties extremely seriously.

He continued, "I have to stay on top of my game. No distractions."

"You're boring," she teased gently.

"In my world, boring is good. Something's gone very wrong when my work gets exciting."

She could see his point. And she couldn't very well get mad at the guy for wanting to protect her life. Still, she sighed. "I'll make up the sofa while you patrol and stuff, or whatever it is you do."

"You won't be sleeping on the couch tonight."

Her pulse leaped. "Why not?" God, she hoped she didn't sound like an eager puppy who'd just been thrown a bone. One of her favorite Madeline C. mantras rolled through her brain. *Make the guy chase you. Don't seem too eager. And never act desperate.* She made out his black form over by the front door. Even if desperate was exactly what she was.

"The first problem with you sleeping out here," he explained, while fiddling with something attached to the doorknob, "is that the sofa is situated right under a large, plate glass window which happens to face the ocean. Not the safest place in the house to be with a cyclone rolling in. And the second problem is that I need to keep an eye on you while you sleep. The bedroom is more secure and will make that easier to do."

She frowned. "Exactly where will I sleep?"

"In my bed."

"With you?" She couldn't stop the hopeful note from creeping into her voice.

He laughed a touch painfully and replied wryly, "No. I'll be awake, patrolling and stuff."

"Patrolling what?"

"The *bure*. The grounds around it."

Oh. She felt like sticking her tongue out at him. Party pooper. She'd been hoping that, if she could entice him to sleep with her, he might come around and reconsider his no-more-fooling-around-on-the-job edict. For a guy who'd planned to just pretend to have sex with her on the beach to draw out the killer, he'd failed miserably so far in the pretending department. Not that she was complaining, though. Never in her life had she experienced sex even remotely that good. Heck, she could learn to really like making love if it was like that all the time!

If only Tom was marriage material according to her grand plan. Then everything would be perfect. He was so damned attractive. Smart and funny and considerate. And responsible.

An adult. The kind of man who would treat a girl right. Her plan definitely didn't stretch far enough to allow for a recovering drunk-cum-beach bum, though.

Emotional security or financial security? How did a girl choose between the two? Could she give up everything she'd built for herself for a man? Her great job, her great apartment, heck, her great wardrobe, and move to a place like this? Tom's *bure* was basically a two-room cabin, albeit a nice one, in the middle of nowhere. And she'd thought her family's farm had been isolated! This place took isolation to a whole new level.

To be with Tom, she would have to be willing to drop out of society completely. She could do without the loud bars and pretentious, repetitive parties. But to be alone? Really truly alone, with only Tom for companionship? That was a big leap from her life in Chicago. Could he make her happy enough to make up for what she would have to leave behind?

Or was she just seeing Tom through rose-colored and inaccurate glasses, after all? Was he any of the things she thought he was? Did he feel for her the way she thought he did? Or was this all an elaborate act to gain her cooperation so he could collect a fat reward for catching the Sex on the Beach Killer? Sure, she got to have great sex with Tom while acting as bait for a killer. But was the sex worth risking her life for? Did Tom give a damn about her, or was she just a prop in his plan to catch the killer?

Insecurity roared through her. In high school, she had never put on airs—or makeup, for that matter—but at least she'd always known where she stood with people. They took her at face value and either liked her or disliked her as they saw fit. Nowadays, she wasn't so sure. She'd stepped into a world of social climbers where everyone put on a good face and nobody showed their true feelings about anyone or anything. Did she dare trust Tom or not?

Was his infatuation with her real at all? Or was it merely something superficial and temporary for him? After all, the sheriff had threatened Tom with jail if he didn't play along and do his best to catch the Sex on the Beach Killer. Maybe the steamy beach sex was only part and parcel of Tom saving his own hide.

Oh, God. What if he didn't have any feelings for her at all?

Agonizing over whether or not Tom returned any of her feelings, she perched on the edge of the couch and did her darnedest not to puke. This was exactly why she'd sworn off real emotions when she embarked on the Madeline C. project. They made a person's palms sweat and threw their stomach into turmoil. She had to be cool, calm and collected at all times, in control of herself and every situation around her to pull off her grand plan.

But she wasn't the slightest bit in control of Tom. If anything, he was the one pulling her strings. All he had to do was snap his fingers—or kiss her—and, oh, how she danced for him. The abandon of their earlier sex on the beach made her blush just to think about it. But she couldn't find it in herself to be ashamed. It had been glorious. And he'd been as blown away by it as she had, or she knew absolutely nothing about men.

Maybe Tom cared for her a little, after all.

Gradually, her panic attack passed as he prowled around the house, setting traps in front of all the windows and doors. Outside, the wind growled and the ocean roared, sounding like lions sent from heaven to rend all that stood before them. It felt like the storm had reached right into her gut and scrambled her innards, tossing her thoughts and feelings into complete chaos.

Here it came. A major Category Three tropical cyclone. Like it or not, she was about to experience her first really big storm. Up close and personal.

The man stared at the *bure* through the thick undergrowth, fingering the razor-sharp hunting knife dangling at his side. How convenient of his victims to lead him straight to this, their secret hideout. As if they could actually escape him on this tiny little rock of an island.

He still had a while before the storm would get bad enough to drive him inside. Plenty of time to wait out his prey. To choose his moment and strike.

Soon, now. He would let them fall sleep, secure in the knowledge that the storm would keep them safe. And then he would unleash the hounds of hell upon them, and let them reap the bitter fruit of their sinful ways. Compliments of the cyclone, it would be days before anyone found their bodies way out here in this isolated cabin. And after the close call of his last kill, he'd learned to be more mindful of his escape from the scene of the crime.

So many islands. So many tropical beaches. So many debased sinners having sex on those beaches. Really, why would men and women do something so foul—in public, no less—unless they actually *wanted* him to find them and punish them for their debauchery? He was happy to oblige them. After all, he was the chosen instrument of vengeance against the damned. And the next two sinners to join the others of their kind in hell soon were going to be Tom Laruso and Madeline Crummby.

Very soon, indeed.

Chapter 9

Tom sat by the bed in a comfortable wicker armchair he'd dragged in from the living room. An oil lamp burned at his elbow on the nightstand, giving off a small but bright light. Enough to comfortably read the tall stack of manila folders that constituted the police reports to date on the Sex on the Beach Killer. He propped his feet up on the edge of the bed, and the results of yet another homicide investigation spilled across his lap, complete with gory photos and grisly crime-scene details.

Maddie slept peacefully on the far side of the bed, curled into a little ball facing him, her fists tucked under her chin, child-like. For as flamboyant a woman as she portrayed herself to be, she slept in a much less outgoing fashion. In his experience with jet-set party girls, they slept as aggressively and selfishly as they lived, sprawled across the whole bed and irritable—even dead asleep—if anyone dared encroach upon their space.

A study in contrasts, she was. She seemed fixated on the idea of landing a rich guy, which seemed so much shallower than the woman herself. In the midst of all her impractical shoes and expensive makeup and slick dancing, he kept catching what seemed like glimpses of a real woman beneath the façade. A woman who fascinated him and appealed to him like no other woman he could ever recall meeting. A woman he had to stay far, far away from if he was going to do his job and protect her life. As much as he'd love to peel back the layers of this complex woman and find her true core, he didn't dare. Not now. Not while a killer was running around trying to kill them both.

The words on the page blurred before him as his thoughts strayed back to Maddie. Why was she so hell-bent on maintaining her uptown, elite socialite image? Apparently, that was the sort of woman who attracted the sort of man she was after. Unfortunately, that sort of man wasn't him. He'd worked for and dodged fake and conniving, marriage-minded women for too long. He had no use for them. He wanted someone real. Someone who'd love him for himself, not his bank account. Someone who enjoyed a great sunset or a walk on a beach, or just sitting quietly, sometimes. Someone who didn't judge people solely by their clothes or their house or their car. He wanted a woman of more depth of character than that.

Hell, at the rate he was going, he wasn't ever going to have to worry about a woman in his life. A bottle of whiskey was likely to end up being his girlfriend, wife and mistress.

He shook himself out of his dismal thoughts and looked down at the file in his lap once more. The couple in this picture had been beautiful. Both of the victims blond and tanned, in great physical shape. A killer would have to be fast and strong to take out a pair like this. Of course, a well-placed knife to the brain stem, wherein most vital life functions resided, would pretty much take out anyone.

A cold chill chattered down his spine. How close had he come tonight to the same fate? He'd been completely oblivious to anything or anyone around them while he and Maddie had made love on the beach. If the killer had wished it, they'd be as dead as the couple in the picture right now.

Tom flipped to the next photo, of the female victim of the latest killing. Pretty girl. Expensive-looking, beneath the crusted blood and pale mask of death. Definite boob job. Even in death, her breasts stood up proud and resilient above her slender rib cage.

The working theory was that the killer stabbed the men first, killing them instantly with a knife to the back of the head. Then, he used the men's dead weight on top of the women to restrain the female victims long enough to slit their throats—a single knife blow down the chin line and then across the jugular and windpipe. Efficient bastard.

He noticed the female victim's hand, flung out as if in supplication. Nice manicure. He liked women's fingernails natural, himself. The whole lacquered, square-tipped claw bit did nothing for him. They seemed so…plastic. Maddie's nails were buffed, but at least they were real. Yet another inconsistency in the whole package.

He'd hate to think that the hottest woman he'd ever bedded was purely artifice. Surely the sex wouldn't be that fantastic if she was a total fake. Could women put on highfalutin airs while screaming their way through multiple orgasms? There wasn't the slightest doubt in his mind she had been faking those, at any rate. He'd felt her body convulse around him, felt the hot gush of her release bathing him.

He stirred in the chair, growing uncomfortable. He had to stop thinking about sex! Although with Maddie sleeping in his bed, her light, sweet scent wafting to his nostrils, it was damned hard not to.

He forced his gaze back to the file. He finished reading the crime-scene report. Pretty much like the others so far. He picked up the next file. The cases were stacked in random order. Next up was the first murder attributed to the Sex on the Beach Killer, a little over four months ago. He flipped open the manila folder and froze at the first picture that greeted him. A red-haired young woman sprawled on her side, naked and dead in all her glory. Beside her lay an equally dead young man. Both of them looked to be in their mid- to late-twenties. But what riveted his attention was the way the dead woman's back arched unnaturally. He'd seen a pose like that before. Exactly like that. *Arielle.*

He turned quickly to the autopsy report on the female victim and skimmed through the details. Ah, here was the bit he sought.

…victim shows extreme rictus of the spinal column, most likely an autonomic nervous system response to a single knife wound to the base of the skull…

The medical examiner in Arielle's case had told him off the record that Arielle probably had arched backward in extreme pain. The cops assumed that her stalker was torturing her when she died, hence the pose in death. No one had ever said anything to him about a knife wound as the cause of death. Particularly not one to the base of her skull. But Lord knew, her body had been all but unrecognizable as human, let alone female by the time the killer had finished slicing her up. The Malaysian authorities had told him by way of comfort that most or all of the mutilation appeared to have been performed postmortem.

He went back to the photos in the front of the file. In this case, the guy's throat gaped open from a horizontal gash, the ends of his esophagus and trachea protruding from the black wound like gray sausage casings. Why the change in M.O.? In all the other killings, the guy had gotten it to the back of the head and the girl had gotten the slit throat. Why the reversal in this case? And then the obvious answer hit him. The girl had been on top when this couple had been having sex.

Arielle used to brag about liking to be on top when she had sex. She said she liked the power of it. The control. He'd over-heard occasional complaints from her boy toys about how rough she was in the sack with them.

Maddie stirred, and Tom looked up. Her eyes flickered open briefly. He nodded at her, and she smiled back, as sleepy and content as a kitten. Her eyes drifted closed once more. A smiled spread across his face. She'd just been checking to make sure he was still there, still looking out for her. Some-thing warm and protective washed over him. *Sweet dreams, little Maddie mine.*

His gaze returned to the pictures of the dead woman. Her hand was frozen in a claw by her ear, reaching backward awk-wardly as if to grasp the blade in her neck and pull it out.

Dear God. *Just like Arielle.*

Was this how Arielle had died? From a swift blade to the back of her head?

If she hadn't been by herself when she'd died, had been having sex with someone at the time, on a beach, he'd wonder if the Sex on the Beach Killer had murdered her. But then, Arielle had been alone...*as far as he knew.*

She hadn't died on a beach, either, and the Sex on the Beach Killer had done his work strictly on beaches. Arielle's body had been found onstage at the giant soccer stadium where she'd been scheduled to perform the next night. No one could figure out why she'd gone there—it was completely out of character for her to indulge in anything faintly resembling rehearsal more than four hours before a show.

There had been a beach nearby, though. How near? Near enough for the killer to have stretched his rules? The stage certainly had qualified as a public, exposed place. Tom sorted urgently through his memory. The stadium sat maybe two blocks away from the Pacific Ocean. Close enough to a beach to send warnings humming low in his gut.

Arielle had succeeded at sneaking out on her guards twice before the night she'd died. Both times she'd gone to the wildest disco in town and partied her fanny off. The hangovers both times had taken her days to sleep off.

So why the inexplicable trip to the venue that last night? Right from the beginning, the question had stuck in his craw. But for the past six months he'd been too drunk to give it serious consideration. Now that he was sober again, the old questions crowded forward, demanding attention.

Arielle had been a wild child, but she'd always taken her career seriously. She never got wasted the night before a performance. Especially not a big one. The show scheduled for the night after she died had been the kickoff to the Asian leg of her world tour. It was a full house with sixty thousand tickets sold and scores of journalists scheduled to cover it. If she'd stayed true to form, she wouldn't have gotten passed-out drunk that last night. But she might have picked up some random guy and taken him down to the stadium to show him the elaborate show set…maybe to prove she was really Arielle…maybe to hump him on stage for kicks…

He hadn't been privy to the majority of the police investigation. He'd briefly been a suspect himself; hence he hadn't been allowed access to the details of the case. By the time his alibi was established—he'd been off duty that night, having dinner and trading war stories with a buddy from his days in the Secret Service—a court order had been issued sealing all details of the case to everyone but the investigators working directly on it. The press coverage of the murder had been beyond sensational, and he couldn't blame the family or the publicist from Arielle's record label for their request of the judge. But, it had meant he never got the lowdown on what had really happened.

His mouth turned down cynically. Apparently, it had been more vital not to negatively impact the surge of sympathy sales of her records than it had been to let trained security operatives, who knew the victim extremely well, help the police with their investigation. Nope, mustn't deprive Arielle's parents and producer of the last few millions they could wring from the teen cash cow before she dried up once and for all. Sad, really. Maybe the ongoing feeding frenzy by her family and supposed friends upon her success helped explain why the rock star had snuck out and helped along her self-destruction.

The folder slipped out of his lap and hit the floor sharply enough to make him jump. He bent down thoughtfully to pick it up. What if Arielle wasn't alone that night at the stadium? What if she'd gone there to have sex with some guy she'd picked up?

What if the Sex on the Beach Killer had stumbled across them? Arielle would've undoubtedly picked up a random boy toy in some public place, likely a disco or a bar. The killer could've spotted them there, maybe followed them to the stadium. Had the cops canvassed all the clubs on the beach strip to see if Arielle had been in one of them?

The club owners wouldn't necessarily be forthcoming

about Arielle picking up her killer in their club. Bad for business. If the police hadn't pushed that angle hard, odds were they hadn't gotten even part of the truth, let alone the full story.

The enormous set of light and sound special effects had already been erected for the concert, the raised platforms wired and ready for the sound equipment to come in the next afternoon. A soccer stadium was just as public, if not more so, than a beach. The murder site had been a *stage,* after all. What better place to symbolically murder a pair of sinners?

Tom lurched up out of the chair, swearing, heedlessly dumping the files onto the floor. He rushed into the living room, yanking out his cell phone as he went. He had to call the Malaysian police! Find out if Arielle had been stabbed in the brain stem. If she'd been at a club earlier that night. If there was any evidence she hadn't been alone. If she'd had sex…

The police prefecture in Kuala Lumpur was still on his speed dial list. He punched in the number. His phone beeped to indicate that the call had failed to go through. He swore under his breath. When a dozen more tries failed to produce a connection, he reluctantly gave up. The island's cell phone tower must already be down.

He eased back into the bedroom and quietly picked up and restacked the files. He blew out the lamp, plunging the room into darkness. Too restless to sleep, he slipped outside into the stormy night. To say it was raining didn't capture the ferocity of the deluge pouring down from the heavens. Hello, Kato. The wind gusted strong enough to knock him off balance and he hugged the building, using it for protection from the brunt of the storm.

He did a quick circuit around the *bure.* Nothing out of place. Man, the rain was really coming down. He'd never seen anything like it. In under a minute, his T-shirt was plastered to his skin and he hadn't even stepped away from the relative shelter of the *bure*. Bending low, he ran for the jungle, palm trees flailing wildly overhead. A massive sheet of rain blew in, slamming into his back and driving him into the fringe of trees. A large, dark shape appeared to duck and turn ahead of him, driven inland before the storm just as Tom was being shoved shoreward.

Startled, he squinted into the darkness, trying to make out what he'd just seen. Was that only a shadow, a trick of the night? Or had there been someone there? The rain eased for a moment, and he peered into the gloom. No one there, now. Was his mind playing paranoid tricks on him? He crept forward until he found a stump to crouch behind. He eased down onto his belly in a prone, shooting position and went perfectly still, watching. The storm roared all around him, and the ocean sounded like it was trying to claw its way up the cliff to the *bure*.

Exhilaration filled him. The night's wildness was contagious, calling to something primal buried deep within him. The rain and wind flowed over him and through him, and he became part of the storm. It was a heady thing.

And then a voice intruded on the night. High, scared and calling his name. He leaped to his feet, swearing violently, and sprinted for the *bure*.

He burst around the corner, and Maddie stood in the doorway, her white nightshirt stark against the blackness whipping around her. In one movement he swept her into his arms, lifted her off her feet and carried her inside. The wind slammed the door behind them. The relative silence inside the house was a shock to his senses.

"Intruder?" he bit out.

"I don't know," she answered breathlessly. "Do you think there is one?"

He let out his breath in a huff of irritation. "No. Why did you yell for me?"

"I woke up and you weren't here. I got scared."

"So you went outside in bright-white clothing that makes a perfect target of you, and shouted at the top of your lungs, so anyone within shooting range of you would know of your presence and exact location?" His voice rose with each word until he was nearly shouting. Panic squeezed his chest until he could hardly breathe. Not again! He couldn't let another young woman die on his watch! He was still too raw from looking at the crime-scene pictures earlier to contemplate losing Maddie without freaking out.

She replied altogether too reasonably, "But he kills people on beaches. Pairs of lovers. I wasn't on a beach and I was alone."

"He thinks we've seen him. That changes everything. He'll kill you and me both whenever and wherever he gets an opportunity. He'll gladly change up his M.O. to nail us. A killer's a killer, no matter how he does it."

Her eyes went big and round and black. He made an exasperated sound and stepped forward, sweeping Maddie into his soaking wet embrace. "You scared the living daylights out of me. Don't leave the house by yourself again. And don't shout like that unless you're actually in mortal danger, okay? My heart can't take it."

She sighed against his chest. "I've heard that's what happens when you get old. The heart goes first."

Equal parts surprised and irritated, he laughed. "I'm not old, dammit." But then an alarming thought occurred to him. Maybe that wasn't how she'd meant that comment about hearts going. Had she been talking about love?

Him? Losing his heart to a woman? Particularly a high-maintenance fashionista like her? Nah. Not possible.

Reluctantly, he turned her loose. "I'm getting you all wet. And you've already had a shower tonight. I wouldn't want a fragile young thing like you to catch a chill. It might turn into whooping cough or some other horrible childhood ailment."

"Childhood? You think I'm a child?" she exclaimed.

"If the shoes fits…"

She headed for the bathroom, muttering under breath and casually—definitely deliberately—stripping off her night-shirt as she went. The tease. He shouldn't watch. He didn't need the temptation. But as the fabric gave way to soft, satiny flesh, he devoured each and every tantalizing inch of it. Lightning flashed through the cracks in the boarded-up shutters, revealing her sassy, skimpy, bikini panties with a red heart embroidered on the right rear cheek.

He watched that sexy little heart twitch all the way to the bathroom, completely unable to tear his eyes away from it. *You are in trouble, old man. Serious, serious trouble.*

Dry once more and sporting her only remaining night wear—a sexy little black teddy—Maddie was roundly disappointed when Tom merely tucked her into bed with a chaste kiss on her forehead and then backed away from her. It was sweet, but she'd been hoping for more from him. She was wearing black satin with peekaboo lace in all the right places, for heaven's sake. But, no. The guy wasn't interested. Wash her up on a beach half dead, wearing shredded clothes and no makeup, her hair plastered to her head with salt water and seaweed, though, and the guy was all over her. What was up with that?

That man was really starting to get on her nerves. Of course, he was also really starting to get under her skin. No matter how much of him she got, she still wanted more. And that was totally unlike her. She'd been highly selective in the men she went to bed with in Chicago. After all, a girl couldn't afford to get the wrong kind of reputation and still expect to land a perfect husband. She'd carefully picked lovers she thought could give her the kind of sophisticated sexual experience a rich husband would expect from a wife. And although their technique had been acceptable, the few men she'd been with had left her feeling cold.

Not so, Tom Laruso. Oh, no. He'd curled her toes and all but set her hair on fire. And he was by far the most unsuitable man she'd ever met, let alone had sex with. Temporary insanity. That was it. It had to be a result of her near-death experience. Waterlogged brain. Post-traumatic shock. *Something* diagnosable.

Except, a tiny voice tucked in the farthest corner of her mind whispered that perhaps she was entirely sane to have fallen for him. For the first time in a long time.

Deeply disturbed by the thought, she pretended to go to sleep and watched from behind slitted eyelids as he relit the oil lamp, sat down beside it and picked up the thick pile of folders he'd been reading earlier. His concentration was intense enough that she was able to open her eyes fully and watch him as he studied the Sex on the Beach Killer's files without him noticing her scrutiny. He radiated intelligence. Competence.

Since when? He was the unshaven reprobate who only sobered up long enough to fly a floatplane between islands now and then to make enough money to buy booze. The man beginning to emerge from his enforced sobriety stood in stark contrast to the beach bum she'd first met. Which version was the real man? If she asked him, he'd no doubt make some off-handed comment that neatly avoided answering the question.

Regardless of which version of Tom Laruso was the real deal, she had to wonder how in the world a man like him had ended up out here on the edge of nowhere, doing his damnedest to drink himself into oblivion.

He shut a file and closed his eyes, pinching the bridge of his nose.

She spoke quietly. "Why don't you come to bed? You look tired."

Proof of the depth of his fatigue was the fact that he didn't jump when she spoke to him. Instead, he sighed and murmured, "It's got to be here somewhere. I just have to find it."

"Find what?"

"I don't know. Something. A clue. Some little thing that will give me an edge over this guy."

"The way I hear it, you already have a big edge on him in training and experience."

He glanced up at her for a moment. It was the barest instant, but it was enough to bring her straight upright in bed. The misery and self-recrimination swimming in his black gaze were horrible to look at. She blurted, "What's wrong?"

"I beg your pardon?" he replied cautiously.

She climbed to her knees and asked urgently, "You heard me. What put that look in your eyes? That blackness? What drove you to this island? To the whiskey bottle in that cabinet over there?"

"Sorry. That topic's off-limits. Next subject?"

She crawled on her hands and knees across the mattress. An alarmed look on his face, Tom kicked his legs to the floor. His chair thumped forward onto all four legs.

"What? Are you going to run away from me, Tom? You can't. You promised Sheriff Marquez you'd look after me. Keep me safe. It's what you do. It's who you are!"

"Not anymore!" he retorted.

"Why the heck not?"

He surged up out of the armchair as if he might, indeed, bolt from the room.

She forcibly calmed herself, breathing deeply until her voice came out reasonable and comforting, the same way she did back home on the farm when an animal was hurt or scared. "What are you afraid of?"

"I already told you. I don't want to talk about it."

"It looks to me like it's high time you talked to someone about it. Why not me? When the cyclone is over and this killer is caught, you don't ever have to see me again if you don't want to."

"You don't know what you're asking."

"And I won't until you tell me. I'm game if you are."

"No."

She shrugged. "It's your call. You and I are going to be cooped up in this house together for a very long time with very little to do except make love until neither of us can stand up…oh, wait…and talk. If I needle you about what you're brooding over nonstop for the next week you'll break eventually. I'm patient. I can wait you out."

He scowled, spun away from her, and without further ado, stormed out of the room.

She sighed. That hadn't gone well. But she was right. He did need to talk about whatever was eating at him. Too wound up to sleep, she plopped down in the middle of the bed, sitting cross-legged. Idly, she picked up the folder off the top of the pile on the nightstand and opened it.

Oh. My. God. Two naked people sprawled all over an eight-by-eleven glossy photo before her. Two *dead* naked people. With blood all over them. She slammed the folder shut, breathing hard. That was the most horrific thing she'd ever seen. She squeezed her eyes tightly shut, but the image burned behind her eyelids, as bright as day. Damn. It was indelibly printed on her memory now. She might as well look at the stupid thing again. Reluctantly, she reopened the file. Pointedly ignoring the grisly pictures on the left side of the folder, she started to read the notes and reports carefully collated on the right.

As long as she didn't think about the victims as actual living, breathing people, she was able to read the police report with a certain amount of detached interest. Particularly fascinating was the FBI profiler's report on the Sex on the Beach Killer. The murderer sounded like a real sicko. How could someone as twisted as this guy not be completely obvious to anyone who met him on the street? It made her wonder if she'd ever innocently bumped into or chatted with someone whose inner life was this turbulent and violent. *How creepy was that?*

The FBI profiler believed that the killer spent time watching his victims prior to closing in for the kill. He might even watch them have sex before he killed. Okay, now that really creeped her out. The idea of this guy watching her and Tom make love positively made her skin crawl. No wonder Sheriff Marquez was so hot and bothered to get this guy off the beaches, dead or alive, as soon as possible.

The police reports didn't inspire her, in the slightest, to run down to the beach and act as bait to draw this guy out. In fact, now that she really knew what he was and what he did, the very idea scared her half to death. But, if Tom needed her assistance to nab this guy, how could she not help him?

Tom bumped into something in the outer room and his quiet oath drifted into the bedroom. The sound comforted her. She wasn't alone in facing the Sex on the Beach Killer.

Wearily, she gathered up the scattered files and piled them in Tom's armchair. She shimmied down under the covers and listened to the storm rage outside. The thatched roof and heavy cinder block and stucco walls muffled Kato's fury. But a certain shiver in the walls announced that the storm's intensity was building. It was more than a little unnerving.

Eventually, she slept, albeit restlessly, her dreams beset by bloody images of dead people making love. Sometime in the wee hours of the night, she roused enough to be aware of a big, warm, comforting body crawling into bed beside her and drawing her close. She snuggled against Tom with a sigh of contentment and went back to sleep, more calmly this time.

Sometime before dawn, two things happened simultaneously. A tremendous racket of noise exploded, like a car alarm on steroids. The high-pitched electronic tone screamed deafeningly. The second thing that happened was Tom flew out of the bed, ripping his arms from around her and disappearing so fast she barely knew what had happened.

"Stay put," he barked over his shoulder. And then he was gone, slipping through the door into the living room, the blocky shadow of a gun clutched in his fist.

She cowered under the covers, waiting in an agony of suspense as each minute took an hour to tick past. Why hadn't he called an all-clear yet? It only took a few seconds to check out every nook and cranny of the whole house. Had he gone outside again? Great. Here she was, scared silly and all alone, and he was God-knew-where crawling around the jungle, playing G.I. Joe.

The window shutters rattled. Rattled again. And then a scratching noise issued from the vicinity of the bedroom-shutter latches. Oh, God. Was that someone trying to get in through the window?

She gazed fearfully at the black rectangle in the wall. It was plenty big enough for a grown man to climb through and only about waist-high. If that was the killer out there, he'd have no trouble coming in to get her! One of the shutters groaned open a few inches, the nails holding it shut squealing their protest as wet wood released them reluctantly.

Ohgodohgodohgod. She rolled away from the window, out of bed and onto the cold, hardwood floor, continuing her motion until she was wedged underneath Tom's king-size bed. Wasn't this the first place a bad guy would look for her? Of course, if the bad guy had gotten past Tom, hiding in an obvious place wouldn't be the worst of her problems.

Was Tom out there somewhere, lying cold and wet and hurt? *Dead?* What was happening? Silent screams echoed in her head. Tom had to be okay! She *needed* him!

The shutter creaked again, the nails stubbornly fighting to hang on to the window frame. The wind howled and rain hammered against the house, and her heart all but burst out of her chest with terror.

An eternity passed. She strained to hear something, anything to let her know what was going on. Her knees and elbows started to hurt, and she wriggled cautiously into a more comfortable position—comfort being a relative thing while crammed into a virtual pancake. Her hand bumped against something cold and smooth.

An acrid, familiar odor filled her nostrils. Whiskey. She groped in the dark and her fingers closed around the neck of a bottle. She grasped it in the darkness. It was a sharp reminder that her life rested in the hands of potentially unreliable man. Reversing her hold on the bottle, she clutched its neck like a cudgel. It wasn't much as weapons went, but it was better than nothing.

Something moved past her hiding place. A man's bare foot. Oh, God. Was that the killer? She shook from head to foot.

"You can come out now," a familiar male voice bit out. Tom sounded as tense as he had moments before the plane had crashed.

"Are you sure?" she croaked. She babbled as she wormed out from under the bed. "The window…someone tried to rip the shutter open…or maybe it was just the wind…but I didn't scream…"

"This time you should've screamed."

She gazed up at him from her belly on the floor. "There *was* someone out there?"

"Yeah."

"You're sure?"

"Yes, I'm sure. I made out some footprints before the rain erased them."

Maddie froze in the act of crawling to her hands and knees. "Is he still out there?"

"You think I'd be in here now if he was?"

"I dunno how you bodyguard types work. Maybe you'd rather stick close to me. You know. Just throw yourself on me and take the bullet." She lifted the empty whiskey bottle. "It'd be faster and less painful than dying inside this."

He scowled darkly. "I haven't had a drink since I met you. Since about twelve hours before I met you, in fact, because I had to fly that day."

"Where's our favorite murderer now?"

"No idea. Took off into the jungle. I couldn't leave you alone and follow him. I didn't want to take a chance of him circling back before I caught up with him and him killing you."

"Will he be back?"

Tom snorted. "Of course he'll be back."

Maddie glanced wildly at the window.

"But he won't be back for a few hours. The storm's really picking up. Hell, to get across the last bit of lawn, I had to crawl on my hands and knees. Couldn't stand up in the wind. It knocked me right over. He'll have to take cover until the worst of this blows past. We're safe for a little while. And we'll be ready for him when he comes back."

Maddie sat down on the edge of the bed. "Wanna talk yet?"

"Nope."

She swung her feet up onto the mattress. "Join me?"

"Soon."

Riigghhtt. She heard the lie in his voice loud and clear. And fear speared through her. He was clearly planning on staying awake and on watch. Which meant he wasn't one hundred percent sure the killer wouldn't be back tonight.

Yikes.

"Get some sleep," he ordered.

As if! With a killer human and a killer storm on the loose just outside? Hah!

She pulled the covers up to her chin, cold to the bone all of a sudden. "Let me guess," she forced out between her chattering teeth. "Next time he won't bother trying to approach by stealth. He'll just come in guns blazing and blow us away."

"Something like that."

Oh, jeez. Tom didn't even *try* to deny it.

She groused, "You could've told me everything was fine, you know. That it was just the wind banging that shutter around and there's nothing to worry about." Gathering a head of steam, she continued, "But, no. You had to be honest and admit that we're about to be massacred like lambs for the slaughter. Like I'm ever going to sleep now!"

"Sorry. I'm in the habit of being honest with my clients. They figure out a little sooner than they otherwise might that I'm an S.O.B., but it makes for fewer hassles in the long run."

"An interesting business philosophy. Piss off everyone up front and don't postpone the inevitable. How's that working out for you, anyway?" she asked with light sarcasm.

He shrugged. "No complaints. Everyone's leaving me alone. And that's what I want."

What was she? Chopped liver? The two of them had been extremely not alone—several times—over the past day. "Are you naturally this big a jerk, or do you have to work at it?"

"Comes with the territory, babe."

Ah. She knew that devil-may-care tone of voice. She spent most of her time these days with people trying to put on grand acts. Heck, she was a master of the art. His flippant comment had been purely calculated to tick her off. Her anger dissipated as quickly as dandelion fluff in the face of the cyclone raging outside.

Calmly, pleasantly even, she asked, "Why are you trying to make me mad? So I'll back off from you? What are you afraid I'll learn about you? Is this professional or personal?"

He made an inarticulate sound that could have been anger or perhaps sheer male exasperation. She knew that sound, too. The macho man retreating deep within his cave to avoid the all too insightful woman who wanted to engage in that most heinous of acts—talking about feelings.

She changed the subject to something less threatening to the big bad scaredy-cat. "How soon do you expect the killer back?" she asked with gentle persistence. She might let him off the hook—for now—from talking about his feelings, but she *was* going to make him talk to her.

Tom gave in with surprising grace, even if she did detect a hint of a huff and a certain slump of the shoulders. "The killer will have to think about the fact that our doors were booby-trapped. That'll worry him. Now he doesn't know what he's up against. He probably figured he'd waltz in here, knife us in our sleep and slip away before the cyclone gets too bad. Then our bodies would rot out here for a week or so before anyone bothers to swing by and see how we're doing. He'll be long gone by then, and no one the wiser that he did us in. He might even have been contemplating getting cute and setting up the scene to look like a murder-suicide."

As shivers of horror crawled up her spine, Maddie tried for a little humor to lighten the moment. "Which one of us would've murdered the other one, I wonder? If I had to bet on it right now, I'd lay odds I'm more likely to murder you than you are me. What do you think?"

A reluctant grin tugged at his shadowed features. "You could try to kill me. But you'd fail."

"Oh, you think you're tough?" she teased.

He snorted. "No, I think you're five foot three and I can break you in half with my bare hands."

And the beauty of it was that she had utter, complete, un-swerving faith in the fact that he would never, ever lift a finger to her. He was just that kind of guy. He might happily drink himself to death, but he oozed the kind of integrity and responsibility that laid down certain lines in the sand that were never to be crossed. Violence toward women being one of those.

She thought about the door alarm. Tried to imagine what the killer would make of it. "All our guy really knows is that there was some sort of alarm connected to the front door. Couldn't any reasonably nice home have a security system?" she replied. "And this is definitely a nice place by island standards."

Tom shrugged. "Maybe. But alarms aren't the norm on a tiny little island like this."

"Yeah, but if you have money or jewelry or some other valuable collection, you might have an alarm system in your house."

"He'll have to consider the possibility. Of course, he'll also have to consider the possibility that I'm not some sex-starved rube he can just stroll up behind and kill."

Maddie pouted smilingly. "You mean you're not sex starved? I'm desolate to hear it."

Tom's eyes narrowed. But if she wasn't mistaken, humor glinted in their depths as he ordered, "Go to sleep."

"Not happening."

"Then lie down and cover up that scrap of cloth you call pajamas."

"You don't like this?" She threw back the covers to reveal her entire gleaming body, reclining in his bed and draped only in skimpy lace and satin. "I chose it especially for you."

His jaw clenched, and if she wasn't mistaken, that was a sheen of sweat on his brow.

"Well, actually, I chose it especially for you to take off me. Like this." She pushed one thin strap off her shoulder to drape suggestively down her arm.

He growled and took an aggressive step forward. Stopped. Swore. "Not tonight. But when this is all over, I'm stripping that thing off you. With my teeth."

Chapter 10

Tom started awake as something large and solid slammed into the wall behind his head. Probably a tree branch. Damn, Kato was really howling out there. He tightened his arm reflexively around Maddie's shoulders, drawing her closer to his side. She murmured in her sleep and snuggled a little closer. What time was it anyway? His head felt as if it had rocks in it. Too little sleep, too little booze, too few answers. And too little time until the bastard would be back. He wasn't ready. He wouldn't ever be ready to face another killer.

Last night's near miss with the Sex on the Beach Killer had been enough to send his blood pressure through the roof. The old diastolic and systolic still hadn't come back down if the throbbing pain in his temples with each beat of his heart was any indication.

Dull, gray half-light filtered in between the bedroom

shutters. Kato's eye wall was supposed to hit sometime in the midmorning. He glanced at his watch. Eight o'clock. Holy crap! He'd slept for nearly four hours! Back in the day, he could go for sixty hours on stim pills and caffeine. Ah, well, he wasn't in the biz anymore. No need for marathon stints on guard. Just one more job to get through. And then he was done for good.

Small problem: Maddie was not just a job.

What the hell he was going to do about that, he had not the faintest idea.

He'd been lucky over the years. Never had run into any serious problems with female clients putting the moves on him. Sure, women climbed all over him when he was off duty, but on the job, he'd always managed to maintain an unbreachable professional detachment. And then along came Maddie. Of course, in his own defense, she hadn't been a security job when he met her and first made love to her.

And she *had* saved his life, after all. Little pieces of that night continued to come back to him, but the whole experience of his plane blowing up around him still eluded him.

"That's some frown you're sporting there, champ," Maddie murmured from beside him.

He glanced down at her, gazing up at him sleepily. Trust glistened in her eyes. He could get used to a woman like her looking at him like that. If she knew what a loser he actually was, that look would go away quickly enough, though.

"And the frown just got worse. Is something wrong?" she asked as she pushed up to a sitting position and plumped a pillow behind her back.

"Nah. Just thinking."

"About the killer? Any new insights?"

"Nope."

"Nope you have no new insights, or nope you weren't thinking about the killer?"

"Has anyone ever told you you're a nosy woman?"

She replied lightly, "The being a woman bit pretty much implies the nosy bit, doesn't it?"

He chuckled in spite of himself. She did have a knack for making him smile.

"So what *was* on your mind, then?" she pressed.

"I want this job to be over so I can get back to my life."

"What life? You and Jack Daniels, together forever?"

He scowled. "I don't recall asking for your opinion of my personal life."

That put some starch in her spine. She went rigid against his side and then pulled away slightly. "If making love the way we have—more than once, I might add—doesn't make me part of your personal life, then you're either the world's biggest hypocrite, or you're the world's biggest bastard. Do tell. Which is it?"

He stared at her, frustrated. She was right, dammit. He *had* given her the right to poke into his personal life. Hell, he'd done his damnedest to crawl inside her soul, too. Like it or not, they had…something…between them. He shied away violently from putting a name to it. But named or otherwise, it was there, nonetheless.

"Well?" she challenged.

"I'm not a hypocrite. At least I try not to be."

"But it's okay to be a bastard?"

"Something like that."

Unaccountably, she smiled. "News flash, big guy. It's not in your nature to be a bastard. You try hard to drive everyone away from you, but at heart you're not a bad person. If you'd give folks half a chance, you'd have friends. Real ones. The loyal kind who'd stick by you through whatever you're going through right now."

"I'm not going through anything," he blurted defensively. She kept doing that—putting her finger on nerves and leaning on them. She could stop anytime, now.

"Sure you are. You just won't tell me what it is you're going through…yet. But I have at least half a hurricane left to weasel it out of you."

"Let it rest."

"Let me in."

"You don't want inside my head, darlin'."

"I'm asking."

"No deal."

She smiled calmly. "I'm not going anywhere, and neither are you. I'm patient."

A seed of fear took root in his gut. She might just win this contest of wills between them. For a little slip of a thing, she was plenty stubborn. Was he ready to spill his guts to someone? To let her inside his fortress of pain and self-recrimination? The very thought made his gut twist in fear.

She threw the covers back and swung her feet to the floor. "Breakfast?" she asked cheerfully.

He got up quickly. "I'll cook. I don't need any ground-up grass and caterpillars, or whatever you health freaks are eating nowadays."

She grinned. "I was envisioning cooking up the last of the bacon and eggs before they spoil, if your refrigerator and stove are still working."

"The stove is propane. As long as the tank hasn't blown away, it should work. I think I heard the refrigerator cut off about an hour ago. The island's power supply has probably gone down, now."

"Excellent. One last real meal before we go into survival mode."

She sounded surprisingly optimistic about the prospect of eating out of cans and boxes for the next week or more. He wouldn't have guessed it of her.

"Do you want to fry the bacon or scramble the eggs?" she asked brightly.

Darned if her perkiness wasn't actually a little bit contagious. Or maybe he'd just been seriously depressed without realizing it. Someone of normal cheer came along, and she seemed like a bloody ray of sunshine.

Cooking breakfast was an exercise in torture for him. He and Maddie kept brushing into one another in the compact kitchen, having to reach around each other to get things. If he didn't know better, he'd say she was intentionally getting in his way and engineering the contact.

They sat down to breakfast in the gray gloom of the shuttered-up *bure* with a candle to light their table. A certain damp chill hung in the air, but the hot coffee Maddie had brewed chased away the unseasonable cold.

The storm howled eerily, the wind singing a deep-throated threat as it tore past at well over a hundred miles per hour. The entire house shuddered when a strong gust came through, and Tom swore he felt a faint, misty breeze driving between invisible cracks in the windows. It was hard not to hold his breath in concern that the house was going to fail under the onslaught. Had the locals not assured him repeatedly that this place would stand up to the storm, he'd be getting pretty tense right about now.

Maddie looked that tense across the table.

He sighed. He ought to do something to distract her.

Reassure her. And without power he couldn't think of much to offer her…except talk, of course. Damn.

"How are you doing?" he asked in resignation.

"Okay. The wind is getting a little hairy, but this house seems to be holding up pretty well."

"Yeah, it'll do fine. It's a solid place."

"Solid enough to stop bullets?"

Well, then. He guessed he knew where her thoughts were straying to. He glanced at the nearest wall. "Yeah, we're fine in here. It's cinder block and stucco construction. Pretty heavy-duty stuff. It would take a high-powered rifle to punch through that. Such weapons exist, but I doubt the killer will have been able to lay his hands on one here, particularly at short notice right before a cyclone strikes. Besides, he'd need to have some pretty sophisticated infrared gear to target us through the walls. I *know* he can't get that on this island."

She nodded, but the haunted look about her eyes didn't go away. Damn. The reassurance strategy hadn't worked. He was going to have to pull out the big guns to distract her.

"Tell me about yourself," he said.

Her eyebrows went up, and if he wasn't mistaken, a bolt of alarm shot through her gaze like chain lightning and then disappeared. A smooth mask settled over her face. Odd. He took a sip of coffee and leaned back to see what happened next.

"Not much to tell," she said cautiously. "I grew up in Manhattan. Live in Chicago. Work for the Secret Traveler, which is a high-end travel agency catering to an exclusive clientele. I'm one of their scouts. I go to likely places, take pictures, write up a report and then go back to Chicago and put together travel packages for interested clients."

"What do you do for fun?"

"Take dance classes," she shot back.

"Touché. What *else* do you do for fun?"

She shrugged and seemed at a loss as to how to answer that for a moment. "I, uh, shop. Work out. Go out with friends. Take in a restaurant or show now and then."

"Sounds dull."

"It is...I mean it isn't as bad as it sounds," she corrected hastily. "I have fun meeting new people. Seeing new things."

"Do you read much? Do anything outdoors, like hike or camp or ski?"

She opened her mouth to answer, then checked herself. He got the feeling she'd changed her answer before it came out of her mouth.

"I like to sightsee. I guess that can be an outdoor activity." She laughed a little and added completely insincerely, "Shopping definitely counts as hiking. Especially when you're hauling a bunch of heavy bags around a megamall."

"Doesn't sound like much fun to me. I prefer trees and fresh air and nature sounds," he replied.

"Is that why you live way out here in the middle of nowhere?"

He shrugged. "I already told you. I wanted to be alone."

"Wanted, past tense? Do you still want to hide from the rest of humanity?"

"I'm not hiding," he retorted.

"What would you call it?"

He stared at her intently. She wasn't going to leave it alone. Relentless, she was. He sighed. "I'd call it early retirement."

"And why did you retire? Both Sheriff Marquez and Nigel seem to think you were really good at what you did. So why up and quit?"

The words just came out of him. He didn't plan it. Didn't think about it. He just answered. "I didn't turn out to be as good as they think."

Maddie froze. Took a slow sip of her coffee, never taking her eyes off him. He could all but hear her mental wheels turning, even over the screaming storm.

"Did you lose someone?" she asked.

He closed his eyes. He should've figured she'd know exactly how to interpret what he'd said. She was no dummy. No, indeed.

"Who was it?" she pressed.

I do not want to do this! he shouted inside his head.

"Let me guess. A woman. Young and single. It's why you freaked out so badly when the sheriff ordered you to protect me. Who was she? Was she shot?"

He swore under his breath and took a big slug of coffee, burning his tongue in the process. He sputtered and grabbed for a glass of cool water.

"As soon as I get access to a computer, I'm going to be able to search for your name and find out everything," she commented. "You can't keep anything secret anymore, you know. Not with the Internet out there."

He closed his eyes. She was right. But if she looked it up later, when she was gone from here, he wouldn't have to face her. To face himself.

"Are you really that scared to tell me the truth?" she asked insightfully.

She should really quit reading him like an open book like that. He *was* scared. But not of her. Of himself. Of looking himself in the eye and admitting that he should've known Arielle would pull some sort of a stunt. That she would be willful and foolish and reckless. He should've stuck around the hotel that night even though he was off duty and had personal plans. He should've listened to his gut.

He started when Maddie squeezed his hand supportively. She'd reached across the table without him noticing.

"Start with something simple. What was her name?" Maddie asked quietly.

"You don't have to treat me like a child. I'm perfectly capable of talking about this without you acting as if I'm going to shatter into a million pieces," he snapped.

She raised one eyebrow. "Then you can tell me her name without biting my head off, can't you?"

He subsided, reluctantly amused. "Her name was Arielle."

Maddie gaped. "The singer who was killed last year?"

"That's her."

"What happened? I heard she was murdered onstage right before a show."

"It was the night before a show, actually. In a big, open-air stadium. The place was deserted."

"Was she shot?" Maddie asked.

"Nope. Stabbed. And mutilated."

"I'm sorry." Thankfully, Maddie fell silent. But his reprieve was short-lived. "And where were you when all this was happening?"

"Off duty. Out to dinner with an old friend."

"And you feel guilty for not being there to save her."

He scowled. When she put it like that, his gut-wrenching self-recrimination sounded rather trivial and silly. "I *knew* something bad was going to happen. I warned her. Told her not to go out. But she didn't listen. And I left anyway…"

"Who was responsible for watching her while you were out?"

"Two of my men. She snuck past them and out of the hotel."

Understanding broke across Maddie's mobile features. "And then she was murdered. When she was out and about on her own. If the press coverage on her was accurate, she was quite a party animal, wasn't she?"

Tom nodded curtly. "Whatever the press said of her was an understatement."

"Is that what she was doing the night she was killed? She was out partying?"

"Probably. I don't know for sure. The details of the case have been sealed. But it would've been like her to hit the clubs."

"And she ran into her eventual murderer?"

Another nod.

"How did she end up dead onstage, then? Was she killed there or was her body taken there?"

Startled, he replied, "That's an excellent question." He cast back in his memory for what he could recall of the few crime-scene photos he'd been able to convince a detective to show him on the sly. Now that he thought about it, he didn't remember seeing pools of dried blood under her corpse. Which would indicate she hadn't died onstage. Could she have been killed nearby—say, on a beach—and then dragged to the stage and left there as some sort of statement by the killer?

Damn, he really needed to talk to the Malaysian police! What if another body was found that night? A young man, also stabbed, his throat slit, maybe washed up on a beach or left somewhere else nearby? An urgent need to know the truth made him so jumpy he could hardly stay in his chair. He shouldn't be this desperate. After all, Arielle was long dead. Solving the case now wouldn't change that. But it just might give him the closure that had eluded him up till now. It was worth a shot. Anything to put this behind him and get on with his life. The next time a woman like Maddie walked into his life, he'd like to be in a position to go forward with her into a long-term relationship.

Whoa. Long-term relationship? With a woman like

Maddie? He blinked, stunned. He wasn't looking for a relationship. Never had been. His work forced him to travel at the whim of his clients, and he'd globe-trotted pretty much continuously for the past twenty years. No time for long-term relationships, and certainly no stability to offer a woman, let alone a family.

"What?" Maddie asked, alarmed.

"You brought up an excellent point about Arielle's murder."

"Is that a good thing?" she asked carefully.

"Yeah. It may turn out to be a lead for the Malaysian police."

She smiled and gave his hand another squeeze. They finished their mugs of coffee in silence.

Then Maddie stunned him again by saying, "You know, it's not your fault. She knew better than to sneak out. Speaking as someone who's been under your protection for a little while, it's obvious you're not trying to make my life miserable. You're only looking to do whatever it takes to keep me safe. She should've listened to you."

What was that sharp pain ripping through his gut? Grief? Rage? Why now? After all these months? All of a sudden his legs were shaking, and a need to break something with his bare hands tore through him. That little twit! What the hell had she been thinking to sneak out like that? She knew Kuala Lumpur was a big city with all the dangers of any major metropolis. She *knew* better than to go clubbing alone! He and his guys had never gotten in her way, never pissed in her Wheaties if she wanted to drink or dabble in drugs or have kinky sex in front of them. They'd never judged her, never commented on her antics, never limited her behavior in any way. They'd only intervened when it was absolutely necessary to safeguard her life. But that hadn't been enough. She still had to rebel. Had to escape…just because she could. It was stupid! Childish! Suicidal! And…and…

His brain hitched as realization broke over him. More than realization. Understanding. Gut deep acceptance of the truth.

...and it hadn't been his fault.

The knowing washed over him like cold rain, cleansing but painful.

"What's done is done," Maddie murmured.

How did she do that? It was as if she picked the thoughts right out of his mind.

Maddie continued, "No second-guesses are going to change what happened that night. You acted reasonably—you warned her, you left guys guarding her, you had no reason not to go out to dinner. And she made a colossally immature and selfish decision that ultimately cost her life. I'd say she's paid plenty for her stupidity. There's no reason for you to keep on paying for it, too."

He shrugged carefully, like his newfound understanding might shatter if he rattled it too hard.

"Thanks for saying that," he mumbled.

He almost missed Maddie's blush as she ducked her head and her hair swung forward to mostly cover her face. She mumbled back, "I hate to see you suffer. It hurts me, too."

It hurt her—huh?

He studied her intently. "What are you trying to say?" he asked bluntly.

She looked up at him briefly and then her gaze skittered away. "I know we haven't known each other for very long. But..."

"But what?"

She took a deep breath and tried again. "But, I've developed strong feelings for you. I don't want you to be in pain. I want you to be happy. I want...us...to be happy."

Us? Oh, crap.

Chapter 11

Almost sick with anxiety, Maddie risked another glance at Tom. He looked nothing shy of dumbfounded. What? Did he think they could share the kind of lovemaking between them that they had without there being any feelings to go along with their incendiary attraction to one another?

"Now would be a good time to say something," she muttered.

"Uh…I don't…I don't know what to…uh…say."

"Not the most encouraging comeback to a declaration of feelings I've ever heard," she said with patently false casualness.

"Well, uh, of course, I'm complimented…" he stumbled through saying.

Complimented? Ouch. Humiliation started a slow burn low in her stomach and spread upward to encompass her lungs and throat, and finally, her face in fiery heat. She stood up hastily and clumsily picked up the breakfast dishes. She turned to flee for the sink just as he reached out to snag her around the waist. The dishes went flying and shattered with a crash of broken glass and broken dreams on the tile floor.

"Oh, God, I'm so sorry!" she exclaimed, not sure what she was apologizing for.

He started to stand. Opened his mouth to speak, but she cut him off. She couldn't stand to hear him say anything else compassionate and crushing.

"Don't worry about it, Tom. I'll clean up this mess. I've got sandals on. You go put on some shoes and I'll get a broom. I'll have this cleaned up in no time," she babbled.

She rushed for the broom closet and buried her head inside it, rummaging around noisily but not finding a broom. A tanned forearm reached past her head and pulled out the broom leaning in plain sight in the back corner of the closet. She stood up, still staring at the interior of the closet. She looked vacantly at nothing until she realized what she was doing and closed the closet door. She turned reluctantly to face him.

Tom wielded the broom with his back to her, already sweeping up the shards of her heart and the mess she'd made on his kitchen floor. She stood there uselessly, watching him take care of everything with the same silent efficiency he did everything. Like dash her hopes for the two of them in a few simple words.

How could she have been so stupid? He didn't feel anything for her! She was bait to catch a killer. Nothing more. They were supposed to make out. To pretend to have gnarly sex. Who could blame the guy if the game of pretend had gotten a little out of control a time or two? Most men would have a hard time restraining themselves when a naked, horny woman came on to them and crawled all over them looking for sex.

And it wasn't as if she'd been crying foul and calling a halt to the shenanigans between them. She'd been all too eager to help spin things out of control. But it had just been sex after all. Nothing more. Right? And that was why she felt violently ill and was seriously contemplating bolting outside and into the jaws of a major cyclone.

She'd been so stupid!

Her face went hot all over again.

Tom looked over his shoulder dispassionately. He asked flatly, "Could you grab the dustpan? It's on the top shelf in the closet behind you."

Numbly, she found the dustpan and held it for him while he swept bits of ceramic and glass into it. She emptied her dreadful mistake into the trash can and stumbled out of the kitchen, away from the ruins of her heart. How could she have fallen for him? He'd never given her any indication that he was interested in anything more than hot sex.

"Maddie—"

She didn't turn to face him. She couldn't.

She knelt on the sofa and peered through the louvered shutters at the raging ocean vaguely visible below through horizontal sheets of blowing rain. One of the palm trees at the corner of the *bure* had been uprooted and lay on its side, mortally wounded. She knew the feeling.

"Maddie."

She ignored him.

"Look at me."

Frowning, she glanced over her shoulder at him.

He stood in front of the couch, his arms crossed defensively across his chest. "What the hell's going on with you?"

Her eyebrows shot up. "I declare my feelings for you and all you have to say is that you're complimented? That's what the hell's going on with me!" She took a deep breath and continued more calmly, "I get the message loud and clear. I'm sorry you're stuck with me until Kato's blown over. I'll get out of your hair as soon as the storm breaks."

"I didn't say I don't want you around."

"I'm sure you do want me around. What guy wouldn't want freebie hot sex from some groupie chick with a crush on him?"

"That's not how I see you," he protested.

She turned fully to face him, her own arms crossed over her bosom. "How do you see me then?"

He exhaled hard. "I can't see you in any light other than being my client until I catch this Sex on the Beach guy."

Her eyebrows shot straight up. "You sleep with all your clients, then? So you're a full-service bodyguard?"

"No! I never sleep with— Okay, not until you. I've never slept with a client before. And you weren't my client the first time we made love."

"No, that was just a case of 'Hey, we made it, we're alive' sex."

"No, it wasn't. I've had plenty of close calls in my life, and I've never randomly jumped into the sack afterward because I'm so relieved to be alive."

"How would you characterize our relationship, then?" she challenged.

"I…we…" He pivoted and paced the length of the room and back, coming to a halt before her once more. "I'm attracted to you. Really attracted to you. And I shouldn't be. The job…my focus…you're screwing up my concentration something fierce. I'm having lousy luck trying to restrain myself with you. I'm sorry."

"Don't apologize to me! I'm obviously the one who should be apologizing for messing up your work so damned badly."

He scowled. "That's not what I meant."

She huffed and asked with thin patience, "Then what, exactly, did you mean?"

"Maddie, you don't want me. I'm a bum trying to drink myself into an early grave. You deserve better than that. Hell, you *want* better than me."

Her gaze narrowed. "What do you mean by that?"

"Look at you. You're sleek, sophisticated, painfully chic and on the prowl for a man. You and I both know you're hunting for a certain kind of man—rich, successful and interested in being a certain kind of wife."

"And what kind of wife would that be, exactly?"

"A trophy wife. A woman who'll look good at business parties, who'll decorate and maintain a beautiful home, who is a visible demonstration of his success in life."

Her jaw dropped. "You think I'm trophy-wife material?"

He looked flustered. "Well, what would you call it?"

She was so offended she could hardly form words. A trophy? Her? She was bright. Fun. Loving. She was so much more than arm fluff to some guy...wasn't she? Or was that exactly what she'd turned herself into?

"Don't get me wrong, Maddie. You're a great lady. Beautiful, smart, witty. Charming. Uh, well groomed. But you have to admit, you're not my type any more than I'm yours. I mean, you're the ultimate uptown girl. You're from New York City, for crying out loud. You live in Chicago. You turn your nose up at anything to do with the outdoors. You don't like a simple lifestyle. You want bright lights and the big city. Noise and action and chaos. I don't want any of that. I've had my fill of it."

His words were a knife straight to her heart. She loved the outdoors! Loved animals of all kinds, trees and starry skies and the deep silence you could only get way out in an isolated forest on a winter evening. She'd liked living on the farm, for that matter. She just hadn't been able to stand the constant financial uncertainty of the lifestyle. But she'd relished the rest of it.

He spoke again, probably out of nervousness or frustration, trying to fill the void left by her silence.

"I can't figure you out. I keep catching glimpses of a woman I think I could spend the rest of my life with, but then all that city slicker stuff takes over and I think we can't possibly have enough in common to build an entire life on."

But that wasn't true! The uptown girl was an act!

And what would he think of her if she told him so?

Then he could add being a phony and a conniving gold digger to her lengthy list of flaws. She was neatly and completely trapped in her own web of lies. In trying to be someone she wasn't, she'd driven off the one guy who'd have loved her just the way she really was.

The irony was almost more than she could bear. She didn't know whether to laugh or cry. But either way, she felt as if she was going to lose her breakfast.

Tom spoke grimly. "It sounds like the eye wall is about here. As soon as it passes, we'll need to head out. I'd like to make another attempt to draw out the killer, now that I know more about his modus operandi. I'll, uh, be in the bedroom until then...reading the Sex on the Beach files."

Coward. She glared at his back as he beat a hasty retreat for his cave to hide from the inconvenient and unpleasantly emotional female. The storm whipped furiously around the little house, buffeting her even through thick walls of block and concrete. Just listening to the cyclone was exhausting. She felt as if she was trying to walk into the wind and losing the battle.

No, wait. That was just Tom she was trying to walk toward and his walls of emotional resistance blowing her back.

Tom emerged from the bedroom a little before noon, silent and stiff jawed. He was carrying a strange-looking armload of towels and linens and clothes. If she didn't know better, she'd say it looked as if he was about to do a load of laundry.

Tense and unbearably uncomfortable, Maddie found herself developing a fascination with the ceiling beams. Yup, they looked plenty solid, even with Kato's worst winds lashing at them. Although she found it hard to believe, the woven thatch seemed to be holding up to the cyclone's fury just fine. Tom opened and slammed several kitchen drawers in search of something. She flinched at each crash.

He disappeared into the bathroom without speaking to her. Which was just as well. She couldn't imagine him having anything to say right now that she wanted to hear. And frankly, she didn't trust herself not to burst into tears if she tried to talk to him. Actually, she felt pretty darned close to tears right now. She swore under her breath. She didn't need to add being a weepy sissy to her list of flaws.

If only he wasn't right. At least she could be mad at him, then. But as it was, she had only herself to blame for wrecking the best thing she'd ever found. She was honest enough with herself to admit that Tom's observations about the fake person she portrayed to the world were spot-on. And darned if he didn't go even higher in her esteem for having made such an insightful observation of her.

Nope. She couldn't blame him a bit…dammit.

He'd blown anything they might have had between them to bits. But worse, he'd blasted her entire grand plan to smithereens. She'd never thought ahead far enough to ask herself the question of whether she really wanted to spend the rest of her life with someone who could be snowed by her act. Could she love a man who was superficial enough only to care about the outward appearances of a person? Who wanted her for a *trophy wife?* Damn, damn, damn.

Now what was she supposed to do? Faced with the prospect of dropping the Madeline C. persona entirely, panic threatened to overwhelm her. It was as scary as heck to consider putting herself out there for all the world to see as she truly was. To expect an intelligent, successful man who met her high standards in a husband, and who had high standards of his own, to choose her. The real her. The her who knew how to milk a cow and drive a tractor and muck a stall.

She *really* didn't want to go back to the farm. It wasn't a bad life. It just wasn't the life she wanted. A horrible feeling of being trapped closed around her.

But which was she more trapped by? Her rural upbringing, or the fake persona she'd so carefully built for herself? Both of them seemed to have her by the neck, choking the breath out of her. She stared at the raging ocean below. Its Category Three–fury made her feel infinitely small and insignificant.

She started as Tom spoke from practically beside her. "Get dressed. Put on that skimpy bikini I saw in your shopping bags."

Her head pivoted around. She stared up at him coldly. "And why would I parade around in practically nothing for you if I'm such a distraction to you doing your job?"

His jaw rippled as he clenched it. Gradually, his facial muscles relaxed enough for him to reply, "Not for me."

She frowned, not understanding.

"We're going out."

"Where to?"

"North Taru Beach."

The name meant nothing to her. She inferred that it was some sort of beach on the north side of the island, though. He wanted to go to a beach *now?* "In case you haven't noticed, there's a major cyclone blowing outside."

"It'll stop soon."

He was infuriating to converse with when he communicated in nothing but sentences with three words or less! She asked as calmly as she could muster, "And why are we going to this beach?" Maybe a why question would force an entire paragraph out of him.

"We're going fishing."

Fishing? What in the world was he up to? They had plenty of nonperishable supplies in the pantry to see both of them through the next couple of weeks. She frowned. "Let me get this straight. You were just sitting in your bedroom listening to Kato, and you said to yourself, 'Self, I think I'd like to go fishing. Right now. In the middle of a major cyclone.'"

Tom blinked rapidly, apparently startled. But still, he didn't break his silence.

"News flash, big guy," she announced, gathering a head of steam. "Fish may bite when it's raining, but they bloody well don't bite when there's a major storm raging. They go sit at the bottom of the pond, out of the turbulence at the surface and wait it out."

He studied her intently. Finally, he said, "And you know this about fish how?"

Suddenly feeling rather three-word sentence-ish herself, she bit out, "My dad fishes. He taught me."

"Ahh, but can the lady bait her own hook?" Tom mumbled.

Her gaze narrowed. "I may not be able to bait a hook for a damn when it comes to catching men, but I can put a worm on a hook for a stupid fish, thank you very much. For that matter, I can tie my own flies and rig my own fly casting pole."

He opened his mouth to say something but she cut him off. "And, I can take a fish off the hook, even if he swallows it, plus I can clean and gut my own fish. I'll have you know I fry up the meanest pan of brook trout east of the Mississippi River." The glare she shot at him made it clear he'd never get a chance to test her skills as an angler or trout cook firsthand, however.

Tom answered curtly, "Today we're not after trout. We're going fishing for the Sex on the Beach Killer. And you're the bait. So put on your bikini and think tasty thoughts. The eye of the storm will be here soon and we'll need to leave as soon as Kato abates. We'll only have an hour or so."

She was just mad enough to relish the idea of putting on the little red bikini and flaunting what Tom had just dumb-assed himself out of having again. She sashayed over to the sideboard where she'd appropriated a drawer last night for her clothes, well aware of exaggerating the twitch of her behind a little for Tom's benefit. *Look all you want, buster. You're not getting any more of this.*

Tom demonstrated remarkable male intelligence and beat a tactical retreat when she turned deliberately to face him and reached for the hem of her shirt. Too bad. She'd have enjoyed doing a wanton striptease for him. It would've served him right.

She was grimly amused when he opened his bedroom door a few minutes later and peered out exceedingly cautiously. She lounged in one of the bar stools, her long legs crossed and prominently on display beneath the T-shirt she'd pulled on over her bikini. Her free foot bobbed up and down in agitation. He eyed it warily and circled well wide of it as he headed for the door.

"The storm's weakening. It's time to go."

She'd been so involved in her private, internal storm that she hadn't noticed the change in the noise outside. But now that he mentioned it, the intensity of the wind was noticeably less. It had gone from screaming to an eerie moan. She almost preferred the former.

Tom opened the door and she gasped as it was all but torn out of his hands. He motioned her to follow him, and with trepidation she stepped outside. Tree branches and palm fronds littered the ground and everything was waterlogged in the extreme. The ground squished beneath her feet as she followed Tom to a shed behind the *bure* that she hadn't noticed before. Several vertical slats of wood siding had been torn off the structure and some roof shingles were missing. Whether Kato's work or just the condition of the structure, she couldn't tell. He wrestled the big doors open and she glimpsed a vehicle inside the garage.

He had a Jeep? Yet he'd made her walk to town the last time they'd gone? The jerk! "Why didn't you drive me to town before?" she demanded.

He glanced up from stowing the pile of clothing and rags she belatedly noticed he'd brought out with him. He shrugged. "You were in such an all-fired hurry to get on with your vacation. I thought you could use a little relaxation. That was before I realized you hate everything to do with nature."

"I don't hate anything to do with nature! Well, okay, I'm not crazy about spiders. But I love the outdoors!"

He swung into the Jeep. Gazed over at her dispassionately. "Could've fooled me."

She swung in beside him with a sigh. She couldn't blame him. "Look. Would you believe me if I told you I'm not always as prissy as I've been coming across?"

He frowned, considering. "I dunno. You seem pretty prissy to me."

She gave him a distinctly unprissy slug in the shoulder with her fist. She commented in an academic tone, "Note the non-girly fist and proper slugging technique."

He winced, rubbing his arm. "Duly noted. Where'd you learn how to do that?"

"I have three brothers. Three big, strapping brothers who like to roughhouse."

Tom's eyebrows shot up. "Remind me never to pick a fight with any of them."

She nodded regally as he eased out of the garage. It took them several minutes to make it down Tom's driveway, such as it was, to the main road. Several times they had to stop, get out and drag debris out of their way. Along the way, he spoke into some kind of walkie-talkie twice. She wondered who he was talking to, but she was still too annoyed to ask.

The sky overhead was clearing rapidly, and patches of bright blue were peeking through the nearly black clouds. How odd was that? They went from a howling nightmare to blue skies and nearly complete calm in a matter of minutes.

Tom seemed to read her thoughts. "If you think this is weird, wait till we go back from blue skies and calm back into the farside eye wall of the storm in a matter of minutes."

She nodded, awed by the towering wall of billowing thunderheads retreating in the distance before them. It truly was a wall of clouds.

Once they hit the main road, it was clear someone had come this way recently. Tom had to weave around downed trees and debris, but they were able to pick their way across the island without having to stop the jeep.

Her pulse jumped as Tom parked in the lee of a sand dune and got out. She jumped out as well and slogged the last few feet to the top of the dune as he spoke once more into his radio. She gasped as she caught sight of the ocean below. Colossal waves like she'd seen on television in surfing documentaries climbed the shore, clawing at the sand with a ferocity that was breathtaking. And deafeningly loud. She felt Tom's presence beside her. Even though he shouted into her ear from a range of about two feet, she barely heard him say that it was time to get the show on the road.

She slipped and slid down the dune face behind him. What was he doing with that pile of rags under his arm? He stopped at the base of the dune, fell to his knees and commenced shoveling sand for his laundry project. She planted her fists on her hips.

"Are you going to tell me what the heck you're doing with that stuff?" she shouted. The wind ripped her words from her mouth. Tom didn't look up and she wasn't sure he'd heard her. She dropped to her knees beside him.

Without looking up, he called back, "Meet Bob. He'll be your date today."

She stared. "Bob?"

"Yup. Handsome, isn't he?"

"Have you lost your mind?"

Tom grinned at her. "Maybe. C'mon."

Bemused, she followed him the rest of the way down to the beach. A half-dozen surfers bobbed up and down in the swells beyond the breakers, some paddling by hand and others being towed by jet skies farther out into the raging surf.

"Are they crazy?" she shouted.

Tom replied, "Nope. Best surfing on the planet is in the eye of a storm like this one. These guys are big-wave riders. They chase hurricanes and cyclones all over the world in search of extreme waves. Most of them are professionals." -

"Professional nutcases!"

Tom grinned. "You don't see me out there messing with Mother Nature."

Maddie shuddered as one of the surfers took a spectacular fall, tumbling down the clifflike face of a wave and disappearing as tons upon tons of white water crashed down on top of him. "Is that guy going to be okay?" she asked in concern.

Tom nodded and fiddled with his armload of clothes. "Yeah, those guys can hold their breath for a couple of minutes and they know not to panic if the ocean pins them on the bottom. He'll pop up once that wave passes. You watch."

She held her breath until, sure enough, the surfer and his neon-yellow board bobbed to the surface. The kid gave a whoop and turned to paddle back out to catch the next wave.

To their left, she became aware of a convoy of golf carts arriving at the beach. She thought she spied the Paradise Cove logo on them, but it was hard to tell at this range.

"What in the world are all those people doing?" she asked as dozens of people piled out onto the sandy beach.

"Same as we are. Wave-watching," Tom replied absently. "Okay. Bob's ready to go. Slip these loops over your ankles and wrists."

Maddie tore her gaze away from the ocean. "What's going on here? What are you up to?"

"I called Nigel and asked him to arrange a field trip over here for his guests to watch the surfers. I'm hoping the Sex on the Beach Killer can't resist the chance to come prowl a beach."

"Are you and I going to give him a show?" Comprehension dawned. "That's why you wanted me to wear this skimpy bikini!"

Tom turned a little red around the gills. "Yeah, but here's the thing. I can't keep my mind on business when you and I together act as bait for the killer. So, I decided to substitute Bob, here, for me."

She frowned. "I don't follow."

"Bob's a life-size dummy made of my clothes. I stuffed him with sand so he's heavy and will move more like a human. I attached an old hairpiece I had left over from an undercover job I was on a few years back. A little of your makeup—I hope you don't mind that I used some of your stuff to draw his face—"

She nodded her okay.

"—but I think the end result isn't half bad. How 'bout you?"

Maddie eyed Bob critically. "He has a bigger beer gut than you."

"Thanks," Tom replied dryly. "But his gut won't show. I need the two of you to lie down by the water and make out. Bob gets to be on top."

"You want me to make out with your laundry?" Maddie asked incredulously.

Tom grinned. "Yup. And you get to act like you're really enjoying it."

Act like—well, heck. She'd been acting like a whole different person for all these months. How hard could it be to act as if she was turned on by Bob?

"What're those loops you want me to put over my wrists and ankles?"

"They're attached to Bob's wrists and ankles. You tie his limbs to yours. Then, when you move, he moves. You put your arm up over your head, he does the same. You put your hand behind your head and it looks as if he's wrapping his arm around your neck."

Maddie laughed at the absurdity of the ploy. "And you really think the Sex on the Beach Killer is going to fall for this?"

Tom nodded grimly. "If he doesn't, you and I have to have sex again for real. And somehow I'm gonna have to see him coming and defend us when I'm totally distracted by you. And I gotta say, babe, so far, keeping my wits about me while you and I are making love hasn't worked out too well."

She couldn't help it. A little part of her was pleased that Tom got so caught up in making love with her that he lost focus on his work.

"I'll be all alone on the beach, then?" she asked in a small voice.

"Well, you'll have Bob. He's not going anywhere."

She scowled.

Tom added, "Never fear, you and I will stay in constant communication. I brought some of the radios and earbuds I used in my protection work. He held up what looked like a pair of cigarette pack–size walkie-talkies. "This is the transmitter base unit. You tuck it in your clothes and use the wireless earbud."

"As small as that is, have you had a look at my bikini? I'm not going to be able to conceal that thing on me!"

Tom grinned. Stepped close. He quickly clipped something small and round onto the top of one of the little triangles covering her chest. And then he reached around behind her, and while his breath teased the short hairs curling at her temple, something cold and hard slipped down the back of her bikini. She lurched forward in surprise, banging into Tom's solid body.

"Easy, darlin'. You'll be lying on your back, remember?

The killer won't see a thing. C'mon. Time's-a-wasting." He glanced to where the guests were starting to fan out from the Paradise Cove carts.

She followed him down the beach a ways to an area with several large rock outcroppings coming almost down to the water's edge. Tom quickly situated her maybe thirty feet away from one of the strings of boulders. He draped Bob over her and adjusted the dummy's limbs. It was uncanny how Bob mimicked her every move. In any other less lethal situation, she'd have found the whole thing hilarious.

"I'll be hiding in the rocks over there," Tom announced. "If you holler, I can be here in three, maybe four, seconds, tops. Okay?"

"Tom, what makes you think this guy will strike in broad daylight on a crowded beach?"

"First, I'm hoping he'll recognize us and desperately want to kill us. Second, I've put you in a secluded spot that can't be seen from the rest of the beach. And last but not least, this guy hasn't killed in a while. I'm hoping his appetite for blood is sharp enough to push him into action."

Tom stepped back, took a critical look at her and nodded tersely.

She nodded back, gulping. And then he was gone. Just like that. She'd had no time to prepare, no time to think about this harebrained scheme. And now, she was lying on cold, wet sand, with a heavy, scratchy dummy draped all over her.

"Radio test. How do you hear me?" Tom said in her ear. She jumped, startled.

"Uh, I hear you fine. Am I supposed to do anything like push a button for you to hear me?"

"Nope. That's a voice-activated microphone I attached to your top. Anytime you talk, I can hear you."

"Great. Now what?"

"Now you make out with Bob."

She writhed experimentally beneath the dummy. "Okay, I feel ridiculous."

"You look ridiculous. Try something simple. Have Bob push the hair out of your eyes."

She reached up and pushed her hair off her forehead.

"That looked great. Bob liked that. So have him wriggle a little."

She wriggled as ordered. "If you giggle at me, Tom, so help me, the Sex on the Beach Killer isn't going to be your biggest problem."

"I don't giggle," he retorted indignantly.

"Fine. No laughing, snorting, guffawing or other expressions of humor out of you. Got it?"

"Yes, ma'am," he replied drolly.

"C'mon, Bob. We're out of here—"

"All right, all right," Tom replied, laughing openly now. "I'll do my best to control myself."

They settled down, with Maddie moving around underneath the dummy just enough to make the thing look alive. Tom, hidden in the rocks, reported in every few minutes from his hidden perch. A few resort guests strolled by in ones and twos. Maddie felt like a total slut, making out for them, even if it was with a dummy. But after she caught a half-dozen people spotting her and averting their gazes quickly, the worst of her humiliation dulled to mere embarrassment. Eventually, even her embarrassment wore off and boredom began to set in. She turned her head to watch the surfers offshore.

Tom's voice brought her sharply back to the moment. "Hey! We're trying to catch a killer here. He only comes out to nail lovers. And I think he only attacks them when they're going at it madly. You've got to put your heart into this."

She sighed. Her heart. Right. That was the problem. Her heart was far too involved with Tom Laruso.

"Bob's crazy for you, Maddie. You're driving him out of his mind with desire. He wants to devour every inch of you and then start all over again."

She blinked. Was that how she'd made Tom feel? The possibility started heat building low in her belly. Tentatively, she pulled the dummy closer and kissed his mouth. Or at least where a mouth would be if he had one. Oh, for crying out loud. She was kissing a pillowcase and probably smearing lipstick all over her face.

Tom's rich, deep voice caressed her ear. "Have Bob trail his fingers down your body. Slower. Yeah, like that.

"He's cupping your breasts—cup your breast, Maddie. You have to move your hand to get him to move his."

She blinked, startled. She reached up tentatively and put her hand over her right breast. New embarrassment flooded her. As if it wasn't bad enough that she was fondling herself in public, Tom was watching her. She didn't know which was worse.

He was talking again. "Bob's kneading until you make that little moan in the back of your throat—knead, Maddie."

She complied. In desperation, to avoid dying of humiliation, she imagined Tom touching her, cupping her trembling flesh, laving it with his tongue, tugging on her nipple with his teeth. Her fingers strayed across her skin, sending tingling sensations shooting low in her abdomen. She moaned faintly.

"Yes. That moan. Now Bob's running his hand down your body. Over your belly. Now lower. Yes, lower."

She followed his instructions, her back arching in spite of herself in reaction to Tom's husky voice.

"Perfect. Uh, now writhe. Think about sex."

"With you?" she asked breathlessly.

He cleared his throat. "Think about the hottest sex you've ever had."

"That would be with you, by a mile."

"Uh, okay then."

She replayed their encounter from last evening on the beach in her head and suddenly didn't have any trouble at all moving restlessly beneath the dummy, casting her limbs wide with abandon, flinging herself into the moment.

She yanked her right wrist free of the elastic loop. Bob's arm flopped to the sand beside her head. She reached up and circled her arm around his neck, pulling him close. She whispered, "This is how you make me feel, Tom." And then she kissed the dummy with all the pent-up passion and loss and frustration inside her.

Chapter 12

Tom gulped as Maddie all but inhaled the dummy. It was just a pile of rags, but the sexual energy pouring off her practically drowned him. It was all he could do not to go tearing down the beach and take Bob's place this second. He wanted her so bad he could barely stand.

He swore under his breath. The idea of removing himself from Maddie like this had been to help him keep his professional and emotional distance from her. And it hadn't helped one damn bit. The mere thought of her was enough to bring him to his knees. That wasn't how this was supposed to go!

He wasn't supposed to be up here sweating bullets, not only because Maddie was doing things that made him so hot for her he couldn't think. He wasn't supposed to have this panicked feeling lurking behind his eyeballs that something bad could happen to her. Wasn't supposed to want to wrap her up in his arms forever and protect her from the entire world.

Wasn't supposed to be so desperately in love with her he couldn't do his job!

Whoa. Love?

No way.

Yes way.

He swore long and hard to himself while Maddie panted in his ear, whispering of all the things she loved having him do to her. All the things she wanted to do to him.

It was lust he felt. Just lust. Right?

Wrong.

Lust might be pounding through his body, but that had nothing to do with the jumbled emotions pounding through his head and his heart.

Maddie's sweet voice tickled his ear. "I wish you were here with me, Tom."

"I am with you, baby. Right here."

"No. I mean in my arms. Looking out for me. Making love to me. You make me feel safe—" She broke off, as if the idea of being safe with him was new to her. Didn't she understand?

"You'll always be safe with me, Maddie."

"Really?"

"You have my word on it." And in saying the words, he realized he meant them completely. He wanted to look out for her, to take care of her, always. The insight rocked him violently. He wanted to make all sorts of promises to her. The forever kind.

Shocked to his core, he glanced down the beach absently. Nobody approaching at the moment.

He skimmed the binoculars across the line of rocks opposite his position. He'd chosen this spot because it afforded the killer the kind of cover he seemed to like, and it still had plenty of good hiding spots for Tom to lurk in wait for the killer.

So far, there'd been no sign of the bastard. Tom had been sure the guy would come out and trawl the north beach when so many spectators would be here watching the waves. A faint rumble in the east caught Tom's attention. In the far distance, a line of thunderstorms had appeared on the horizon. The rest of Tropical Cyclone Kato.

They were running out of time.

"Can you make more noise, Maddie? We've got to draw this guy out now."

"Assuming…ohhh, yesss…he's anywhere…right there, yes, yes!…nearby, you mean?"

Tom closed his eyes in actual, physical pain. "Keep that up and I'm going to come down there, beat up Bob and take his place."

She muttered, "I wish you would." Tom jumped as she all but shouted, "Oh, baby!"

She was killing him here.

"Yes! Yes! Yes!" And then, as she and Bob rolled around in the sand, she murmured sotto voce, "I'm channeling *When Harry Met Sally*. How am I doing?"

"Outstanding," Tom groaned.

Maddie rolled over, sat up and straddled Bob. She rocked back and forth fast and hard, looking to any observer as if she was humping the poor guy's brains out. Sweat popped out on Tom's head as vivid recollection of what that felt like rolled over him. He was going to have an orgasm, just sitting here thinking about sex with her! Must. Stay. Focused. He clenched the binoculars painfully tight in his left hand and squeezed the butt of his pistol in the other hand until he thought the grip might bleed.

As Maddie and Bob flailed wildly and Maddie moaned and groaned loudly, a flash of movement from the rocks opposite him caught his eye. Hell.

"Maddie!" he shouted in her ear. "Get on your back! Now!"

Tom leaped up and took off running. Time slowed to an exaggerated crawl, each millisecond registering with frightening clarity in his mind. The sand was deep beneath his feet, swallowing his running steps.

Maddie looked up, surprise etched on her face.

The man running from behind the rocks lifted his right arm. Something flashed, dull and metallic, in his hand.

Maddie's shoulder ducked as she leaned forward to roll over.

Tom staggered forward, his right hand taking forever to lift away from his side. Did he dare take the shot? It would be insanely close to Maddie. A few inches off target and she'd die.

The killer leaped. His knife arced downward, plunging into the dummy, which Maddie had just barely managed to yank across her body in time. The blade slashed into Bob's exposed head, and sand poured out of the gash, a macabre parody of what would have otherwise spilled out had that been his or Maddie's skull.

Tom's index finger clenched, pulling through the trigger in a single smooth movement as he sighted down the short barrel of the weapon. *Caa-rack!* Just as the pistol fired, the killer dived to the side.

Maddie screamed.

Dear God, was she hit? Had he shot her?

The killer roared in rage, and suddenly time resumed normal speed, accelerating to a frantic scramble of events that Tom reacted to on pure instinct.

The killer pounced on top of Maddie and Bob, and apparently realized the ruse. A scream of fury erupted from the guy's throat as Tom lowered his shoulder and charged. The impact knocked the guy off Maddie, and the momentum sent the two men rolling down the slope of the beach. Tom lost his grip on his pistol and it flew away.

Glaring from a range of about twelve inches, the killer's blue eyes were crazed. Engulfed in rage. Completely insane. And something inside Tom snapped. This son of a bitch had just tried to kill Maddie! As big and strong as the killer was, Tom was just as big and strong. And as crazy as this bastard might be, in that moment, Tom was a little bit crazier.

The two men grappled, their arms straining, hands grasping and punching, knees jerking, elbows flying.

Tom grunted, "Did you…kill Arielle?"

A maniacal grin twisted the killer's face. "That whore… pranced all over stage half naked…incited indecent behavior…lured young boys to pornography…"

The killer grunted as Tom grabbed his thumb and gave it a hard twist. The killer countered with an elbow to Tom's ear.

"Hell, yes, I killed her…sent her and that gigolo of hers… straight to hell."

Tom was so stunned by the admission that, for an instant, he lost focus on the killer. The guy made a fast move and got his hands around Tom's neck. Cruel thumbs dug into his jugular. *Oh, crap.* In a matter of seconds, the blood flow to his brain would be interrupted and he would pass out. Tom thrashed beneath the guy, struggling to throw the madman off him.

A fast-moving object barreled at them from Tom's right. He felt an impact, but no pain. The killer grunted in surprise. Tom gasped for air as the vice around his neck eased. The spots dancing before his eyes subsided.

A meaty thud of knuckles on flesh sounded above Tom, and warm wetness sprayed his face.

A female voice grunted, "Leave. Him. Alone." Two more

juicy punches landed, the second accompanied by a crunching noise like bone breaking. "I love him, you bastard!"

Oh, no. Not Maddie. She hadn't joined the fight, had she? This guy would kill her!

On cue, the killer let go of Tom and twisted to attack this new threat. And therein lay his fatal mistake. Tom let fly with his right fist, putting behind the blow every ounce of his love and panic for Maddie, who'd recklessly dived into this fight to the death. His fist landed on the killer's left temple.

It wasn't a pretty blow, not boxing ring or Hollywood-movie perfect in its target, but it had the intended effect. The killer's eyes rolled up into his head even as he toppled over in the sand and went still.

Maddie flew at their attacker, pummeling him with her distinctly un-girly fists.

Tom shoved the guy's inert weight off him and leaped to his feet. He looked around fast and spotted his pistol half buried in the sand. He pounced on it and scooped it up. Pivoting around, he raised the weapon and aimed it at the prone killer.

He was riveted by the sight that greeted him.

Maddie knelt by the killer with tears streaming down her face. Between blows to the killer's head and body, she sobbed at the assailant's crumpled form, "Don't you get it, you jerk?" *Thwack.* "I love him." *Thwack.* "I'm not a city girl, dammit." *Thwack.* "I was born and raised on a farm! I love nature!" *Thwack.* "I dressed up and moved to the city to marry a—" *thwack* "—rich guy because I was so scared of being poor!" *Thwack.* "But I don't want to be a trophy wife." *Thwack, thwack.*

A smile tickled at the corners of Tom's mouth. He stepped forward. "Honey, I think that's enough punching-bag time for you."

"He tried to—" *thwack* "—kill you!"

Tom said gently, "I'm just fine, Maddie. You can stop hitting the bad man."

"But—"

He reached down and drew her to her feet. She turned and buried her face in his chest, sobbing in earnest, now. "I was so scared."

"You were incredibly brave, darling. When he jumped at you with that knife, I thought my heart would stop."

"That's not what scared me," she sniffled against his chest. "I was scared when you jumped him. I thought you were going to get yourself killed trying to protect me."

He leaned back enough to stare down at her. "What? Didn't you think I could take care of myself? Honey, I'm a black belt in four different martial arts and was a national wrestling champion in college."

"I didn't think. I just saw you in danger and I," she said and sniffed loudly, "sort of flipped out."

"Yeah, I noticed."

"Are you mad at me?" she asked in a small voice.

"That you went ballistic when you thought I was going to die? How can I be mad at you for that? I did the exact same thing."

"Really?" A tentative smile sparked in her watery eyes.

"Yeah, really," he answered gruffly.

"You know what that means, don't you?"

He gazed deep into her eyes, a slow smile spreading outward from his soul to encompass his entire being. "I guess I do. It means I'm plumb-crazy, slam-dunk, head-over-heels in love with you, Maddie Crummby. Fussy makeup and prissy clothes and goofy shoes and all."

"My shoes are *not* goofy!"

"Well, they're damned impractical."

She smiled up at him slyly. "Yeah, but they're sexy, aren't they? You like my toes peeking out at you, don't you? You like my pedicure and the little flowers painted on my toenails. Admit it."

He tucked her under his left arm as they stepped back from the unconscious killer. The commotion of their fight had drawn the attention of people down the beach, and a number of them were coming to investigate. Hopefully, one of them would be Herman Marquez or his deputy.

Silence fell over him and Maddie, punctuated only by the rhythmic crash of the ocean beside them. The wind was starting to pick up again, hinting at the storm to come.

Maddie murmured reflectively, "I thought landing a rich husband was the only way I'd ever be safe. I never realized that having someone care about you enough to die for you is a million times safer than a fat bank account."

Understanding dawned. She wasn't a gold digger after all! She just wanted financial peace of mind. That he could give her. "Honey, I've worked nonstop for the past two decades, all expenses paid and have banked practically my entire salary. And I was damned good at what I did. I didn't make chump change. I've got more money than I know what to do with."

She absorbed that for a moment, then asked, "Do you miss your job?"

"Nope. As of right now, I'm officially retired."

She snuggled against his side, and he savored the warmth of her body nestled trustingly against his. He needed only one protection job, now. This one. In return for keeping his heart safe, he'd joyfully protect and provide for her for the rest of their days. Something peaceful unfurled inside him. Like a sail catching the wind, it filled taut and stretched, straining at its moorings until he thought it might break free and fly. And then it dawned on him. That sail was his life. And Maddie had filled it to overflowing.

Without looking away from his motionless prisoner, Tom murmured, "Okay, fine. I admit it. I like your toes. I particularly like sucking them and licking between them and hearing that funny little catch in the back of your throat—"

"Tom! Stop that! There are people coming to help us and I'd hate to embarrass them all by having to throw you down right here on the spot, rip off all your clothes and have my way with you in front of all of them."

He grinned and gave her an affectionate squeeze. "I'd like to see you try."

"Later," she murmured under her breath as the first people caught sight of Tom's weapon and pulled up short.

"It's okay, folks," he called. "Show's over."

"For now," Maddie murmured under her breath.

"We just caught the Sex on the Beach Killer," he called. "The situation's under control."

"Until I get you alone," she added sotto voce.

"Could someone go find Sheriff Marquez or one of his guys, and maybe a length of rope while you're at it?"

"Ooh. Rope. Gonna get kinky on me, are you? Gonna tie me up? Whatever will you do with me, then?" Maddie murmured.

A visual image of that roared through his brain, erasing all rational thought and sending blood pounding through regions of him that didn't need any more pounding blood just now. "Stop that," he laughed under his breath.

"Stop what?" She batted her eyes up at him, in all-sweet innocence.

"You really are a vixen."

She smiled widely and opened her mouth to reply when a

blur of movement startled her. The killer at their feet surged up off the sand, unbelievably fast. Triumph glittered in the bastard's eyes as his knife—forgotten in the sand—glittered in his hand. In an instant, Tom realized he was out of position to defend Maddie against the blow, and there was no time to aim his pistol and fire.

He did the only thing any bodyguard worth his salt could do. In one fluid movement, he shoved Maddie aside and stepped forward into the blow, giving his body to the killer's knife to save Maddie.

An explosion of noise accompanied the killer's body, slamming into him and knocking them both to the ground. Tom felt no pain, just a hot gush of blood across his gut and down his left side. Someone was screaming his name over and over.

Time froze.

He'd done it. He'd saved his charge this time. He'd gotten it right. Peace flowed over him, along with that pulsing stream of blood. All the guilt and recriminations of the past six months washed away. And in that suspended instant of time, he felt gratitude to the killer sprawled on top of him for giving him the redemption that he'd craved. Tom's gaze met the killer's.

The man's pale blue eyes widened in surprise. And then, ever so slowly, they went blank. Dead.

Huh?

Tom moved experimentally. If he'd been stabbed, he sure wasn't feeling it.

A British-accented voice barked, "Everyone stay back!" The screaming stopped.

Tom looked up. Nigel Cumberland was advancing cautiously, a still-smoking pistol held in a shooter's grip in both hands in front of him. The Brit shoved the killer with his foot. The heavy weight rolled off Tom.

"You all right?" Nigel asked tersely.

Tom took stock. "I guess so." He sat up—and was promptly knocked over again by Maddie. Frantic hands ran over his body, and then she collapsed, sobbing, against his chest.

Nigel pressed a hand to the killer's throat. "Dead," he announced.

Tom looked down at himself as he carefully pressed Maddie slightly away from him. He was covered in blood from where the killer had bled out on him.

"I must've hit his aorta," Nigel commented. "Lucky shot."

Maddie piped up, still a little quavery. "I thought you English police don't carry guns."

Nigel laughed. "I'm not a bobby now, am I?"

"Thank God for that," Tom replied. The two men grinned at each other.

Nigel said, "When you radioed me and asked me to arrange this little field trip to the beach, I figured you were trying to smoke out the killer. I grabbed my Beretta just in case." He patted the weapon, now safely holstered at his side.

A new voice rang out from the back of the crowd. "What's going on here?"

Tom closed his eyes in relief. Herman Marquez. He was more than ready to hand this whole mess over to the sheriff and be done with it, once and for all. "Looks like Nigel, Maddie and I bagged a serial killer, Marquez. You don't happen to have a spare body bag on you, do you?"

The sheriff and Nigel took over shooing away the crowd from the corpse.

A gust of wind lifted Maddie's blond hair, tussling it around her face and transforming her into the fresh, natural, breathtakingly beautiful woman he'd woken up to on a beach a lifetime ago. Was it only two days? It didn't seem possible.

Marquez ordered, "Time to head back home, folks. Kato's still got a little blowing to do. Tom, Miss Crummby, I'll need you to come down to the station and make statements as soon as the storm blows over."

Tom nodded. "No problem."

Marquez looked from the killer's battered face to Tom. "Looks like you worked him over pretty good, Laruso. I gather he didn't go down without a fight?"

Tom grinned. "Maddie's the one who beat him to a pulp."

Marquez looked over at her in surprise and back down at the killer. "A tiny little thing like you did all that?"

Maddie shrugged. "My brothers taught me how to fight like a proper country girl. They said it might come in handy someday."

Marquez grinned. "I should say it did." He looked back and forth between them, his knowing gaze dancing with humor. "Congratulations, ma'am. It looks like you bagged your man."

"What are you talking about?" Tom asked in quick suspicion.

Maddie looped her arm around his waist. "Why don't you come back to the *bure* and I'll explain it to you, darling."

A female voice called out from the grinning crowd. "I've got the bridal issue of *Vogue* at the shop. As soon as the storm's over, I'll bring it over to you."

Maddie called back airily, "That would be perfect, Trudi."

He and Maddie trudged up the dune toward his Jeep. "What's this about *Vogue?* The bridal issue?"

Maddie stopped. Turned to face him and looped her arms around his neck. "Breathe, Tom. It'll be okay. I promise not to plan too big a wedding."

A wedding? A moment's panic gave way to a burst of joy

so intense it nearly brought him to his knees. "Really? You'd actually consider marrying a bum like me?"

"You're a lot of things, Tom Laruso, but a bum is *not* one of them. And I assure you, I'm going to do a whole lot more than consider marrying you. I'm going to make you the happiest man on earth for a very, very long time to come."

Wonderment filled him. How on God's green earth had he landed a woman like Maddie? Out here at the end of the world, lost in a bottle of whiskey and looking to die young? Would miracles never cease?

"You have no idea the roller coaster your life's about to turn into, Tom Laruso. Take my advice, big guy—just sit back and enjoy the ride."

"I plan to, Maddie. I plan to."

Epilogue

Maddie walked into the institutionally plain conference room and wrinkled her travel reviewer's nose critically at the décor. But then she caught sight of a pair of familiar, smiling faces and squealed in delight. "Zoë! Alicia!"

She rushed forward and the three women traded hugs all around while Sean "Breeze" Guthrie, Griffin Malone and Tom looked on indulgently.

"So tell me! What have you two been up to these past few months?" But then she glanced at the wedding band nestled beside Zoë's magnificent diamond engagement ring and her gently expanding waistline. "I can see what you've been up to, girlfriend. Just tell me you got that man to marry you *before* he got you in a family way."

"Absolutely. We tied the knot as soon as we got back from doing those last two resort reviews for the Secret Traveler." Zoë smiled affectionately at her husband, who smiled back at her. The sparks flying between them all but set the room's carpet on fire.

"Did Mr. Cameron finally wise up and put you on the Secret Traveler's A-Team?" she asked Zoë.

Her friend nodded, smiling self-deprecatingly. "He said my reviews have a sexy and romantic flair that will really appeal to his customers."

Alicia teased, "It must be all that detailed and meticulous research you and Breeze did to find the most romantic spots at the resorts."

Maddie and Alicia laughed as Zoë blushed fiercely.

In a transparent ploy to distract them, Zoë asked, "How 'bout you, Alicia? How are you settling into life as a stepmother?"

Their friend's eyes lit up with love and contentment. "Wanna see some pictures of Griffin's—our—daughter? She's a real charmer."

Maddie would never have pegged Alicia as the maternal type, but she'd never seen anyone look happier. Alicia glowed from the inside out. Maddie asked, "Have you two set a date yet?"

"For Christmas vacation this year, the three of us are planning to fly to Fiji. We thought we'd have a small ceremony there. Just family and a few friends. Any chance you and Tom can make it?"

Zoë piped up. "They're having the wedding at our resort. It's only about an hour's flight from Vanua Taru."

Maddie hugged Alicia. "Tom and I wouldn't miss it for the world."

"What about you, Maddie? How are you two getting along?" Zoë asked.

"We're doing great. Better than great. He's taken a job as the chief of security at Paradise Cove, and he's building another room onto his place for me."

Alicia asked playfully, "What's it gonna be? A walk-in closet for all your shoes?"

Maddie laughed. "Actually, we're hoping it'll be a nursery before too long."

Zoë gasped. "Are you—"

"Not yet. We thought we'd get married first. The sheriff on Vanua Taru—he's a friend of ours—has agreed to marry us as soon as we get back to the island. We flew to Chicago last week to pack up the last of my things and sell my condo. Good-bye to bitter Midwest winters!"

"Amen to that." Zoë laughed.

Alicia glanced over at Griffin and the pair's gazes met with an obvious and sexy promise. She commented, "Virginia Beach is close enough to the ocean that the winters aren't supposed to be rough. And I have to confess, I like my four seasons."

Maddie teased, "And those seasons would be hot-and-naked, wet-and-naked, cuddly-and-naked and sweaty-and-naked?"

The three women laughed. "Exactly!" Alicia replied.

Griffin Malone spoke up from across the room. "If you three are done catching up, I'm ready to start the briefing."

Maddie and the others moved over to the conference table. She was glad when Tom sat down beside her and took her hand, pulling it into his lap. His thumb idly caressed her palm, sending a flood of images—to act upon later—rushing through her brain.

Griffin, looking as handsome as ever in a dark tailored suit, opened a file at the head of the table. "The case on the Sex on the Beach Killer has been officially closed. Because all of you played a part in stopping him, the Bureau has given me permission to share the details of the case with you. You understand, however, that we must ask you not to share this information with the public or the press."

Alicia cut in. "Isn't he cute when he acts all official like that?"

Griffin threw her an affectionate, if mildly exasperated, glance that promised retribution later. He continued, "The killer's name was Bronson Spindler. He was born and raised in Philadelphia, and the FBI's profile on him was substantially correct in all aspects."

Breeze spoke up. "Way to go, Grif. Weren't you the guy who worked up that profile?"

Griffin shrugged, but nodded. "This guy's mother was a bona fide nutcase. She abused Bronson pretty harshly as a kid. She was obsessed with sex being evil and showed Bronson extensive pornography, then beat him for showing any response to it. I won't go into the details, but suffice to say, she was a monster and created a monster in her son."

Maddie shuddered and Tom squeezed her hand in reassurance.

"Spindler started killing in the United States. We believe he's responsible for three murders here—one in Florida, one on Cape Cod and one in California. He probably believed the law was getting too close to him and moved his operation to the South Pacific. That's just my guess, however."

Breeze snorted. "Your guesses about this guy have been spot-on right from the start. I'd say odds are you're right on this one, too."

"Thanks," Griffin replied. The FBI agent looked over at Tom. "The Malaysian authorities have found a nightclub owner who admitted that Arielle Michilano was in his place the night of her murder. As you conjectured, Tom, she picked up a guy there and the two left together. The club owner was able to pick out Mr. Spindler's picture from a mug book and remembers seeing him follow the couple from the club. The owner thought Spindler was Arielle's bodyguard, in fact."

Griffin took a deep breath before continuing. Maddie blinked. Wow. This case must have gotten to him more than she'd realized. But then, the Sex on the Beach Killer had nearly killed the woman he loved.

Tom tensed beside her as if he sensed what Griffin was about to say next.

"As a few of you already know, the Sex on the Beach Killer took buttons from the clothes of his victims as trophies. We found his collection and have accounted for all of them. Tom, we found a button from the blouse Miss Michilano was wearing when she died. Spindler definitely killed her."

Tom's fingers clenched convulsively around Maddie's, but then slowly relaxed.

She murmured to him, "Are you okay?"

He nodded, a sad but peaceful look in his eyes. "She knew better, and I warned her. It was her choice. Her responsibility."

Maddie smiled warmly at him. He'd come a long way since she'd met him six months ago when he was all but drowning in guilt over Arielle's death.

Griffin filled in a few more particulars of the case, but the briefing didn't take much longer. Everyone stood up, sobered by the information they'd just heard. It was no surprise to Maddie that she and both her friends turned to their respective men for long, quiet hugs.

Finally, that whole, ugly chapter of all their lives was closed. And from the looks of it, all of them were about to embark on pretty spectacular new chapters. Zoë and Breeze were headed back to Fiji and his resort to make a home and start a family—and Zoë got to keep doing the reviewing job she loved. Griffin and Alicia had already built a family and were happily nesting here in the States. And she and Tom— they were putting down roots in Vanua Taru, and nothing and nobody was going to budge them or tear them apart. Not a cyclone, not even a serial killer.

They'd all had the last laugh on the Sex on the Beach Killer. His goal had been to drive lovers apart, to frighten and terrorize people away from love. But instead, he'd created not one, but three killer couples, all of them building a love that would last a lifetime and beyond.

If only Spindler had known what Zoë and Breeze, Alicia and Griffin, and she and Tom knew. True love conquers everything in the end.

* * * * *

The Colton family is back!
Enjoy a sneak preview of
COLTON'S SECRET SERVICE
by Marie Ferrarella,
part of
THE COLTONS: FAMILY FIRST *miniseries.*

Available from Silhouette Romantic Suspense
in September 2008.

He cautioned himself to be leery. He was human and he'd been conned before. But never by anyone nearly so attractive. Never by anyone he'd felt so attracted to.

In her defense, Nick supposed that Georgie could actually be telling him the truth. That she was a victim in all this. He had his people back in California checking her out, to make sure she was who she said she was and had, as she claimed, not even been near a computer but on the road these last few months that the threats had been made.

In the meantime, he was doing his own checking out. Up close and exceedingly personal. So personal he could feel his blood stirring.

It had been a long time since he'd thought of himself as anything other than a law enforcement agent of one type or other. But Georgeann Grady made him remember that beneath the oaths he had taken and his devotion to duty, there beat the heart of a man.

A man who'd been far too long without the touch of a woman.

He watched as the light from the fireplace caressed the outline of Georgie's small, trim, jean-clad body as she moved about the rustic living room that could have easily come off the set of a Hollywood Western. Except that it was genuine.

As genuine as she claimed to be?

Something inside of him hoped so.

He wasn't supposed to be taking sides. His only interest in being here was to guarantee Senator Joe Colton's safety as the latter continued to make his bid for the presidency. Everything else was supposed to be secondary, but, Nick had to silently admit, that was just a wee bit hard to remember right now.

Earlier, before she'd put her precocious handful of a daughter to bed, Georgie had fed his appetite by whipping up some kind of a delicious concoction out of the vegetables she'd pulled from her garden. Vegetables that, by all rights, should have been withered and dried. She'd mentioned that a friend came by on occasion to weed and tend it. Still, it surprised him that somehow she'd managed to make something mouthwatering out of it.

Almost as mouthwatering as she looked to him right at this moment.

Again, he was reminded of the appetite that hadn't been fed, hadn't been satisfied.

And wasn't going to be, Nick sternly told himself. At least not now. Maybe later, when things took on a more definite shape and all the questions in his head were answered to his satisfaction, there would be time to explore this feeling. This woman. But not now.

Damn it.

"Sorry about the lack of light," Georgie said, breaking into his train of thought as she turned around to face him. If she noticed the way he was looking at her, she gave no indication. "But I don't see a point in paying for electricity if I'm not going to be here. Besides, Emmie really enjoys camping out. She likes roughing it."

"And you?" Nick asked, moving closer to her, so close that a whisper would have trouble fitting in. "What do you like?"

The very breath stopped in Georgie's throat as she looked up at him.

"I think you've got a fair shot of guessing that one," she told him softly.

* * * * *

Be sure to look for
COLTON'S SECRET SERVICE
and the other following titles from
THE COLTONS: FAMILY FIRST *miniseries:*

RANCHER'S REDEMPTION
by Beth Cornelison
THE SHERIFF'S AMNESIAC BRIDE
by Linda Conrad
SOLDIER'S SECRET CHILD
by Caridad Piñeiro
BABY'S WATCH
by Justine Davis
A HERO OF HER OWN
by Carla Cassidy

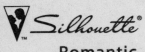

Silhouette®

Romantic SUSPENSE

Sparked by Danger, Fueled by Passion.

The Coltons Are Back!

Marie Ferrarella

Colton's Secret Service

The Coltons: Family First

On a mission to protect a senator, Secret Service agent Nick Sheffield tracks down a threatening message only to discover Georgie Gradie Colton, a rodeo-riding single mom, who insists on her innocence. Nick is instantly taken with the feisty redhead, but vows not to let his feelings interfere with his mission. Now he must figure out if this woman is conning him or if he can trust her and the passion they share....

Available September wherever books are sold.

REQUEST YOUR FREE BOOKS!

2 FREE NOVELS PLUS 2 FREE GIFTS!

Silhouette® Romantic

SUSPENSE

Sparked by Danger, Fueled by Passion!

YES! Please send me 2 FREE Silhouette® Romantic Suspense novels and my 2 FREE gifts (gifts are worth about $10). After receiving them, if I don't wish to receive any more books, I can return the shipping statement marked "cancel." If I don't cancel, I will receive 4 brand-new novels every month and be billed just $4.24 per book in the U.S. or $4.99 per book in Canada, plus 25¢ shipping and handling per book plus applicable taxes, if any*. That's a savings of at least 15% off the cover price! I understand that accepting the 2 free books and gifts places me under no obligation to buy anything. I can always return a shipment and cancel at any time. Even if I never buy another book from Silhouette, the two free books and gifts are mine to keep forever.

240 SDN EEX6 340 SDN EEYJ

Name	(PLEASE PRINT)	
Address		Apt. #
City	State/Prov.	Zip/Postal Code

Signature (if under 18, a parent or guardian must sign)

Mail to the **Silhouette Reader Service:**
IN U.S.A.: P.O. Box 1867, Buffalo, NY 14240-1867
IN CANADA: P.O. Box 609, Fort Erie, Ontario L2A 5X3

Not valid to current subscribers of Silhouette Romantic Suspense books.

Want to try two free books from another line?
Call 1-800-873-8635 or visit www.morefreebooks.com.

* Terms and prices subject to change without notice. N.Y. residents add applicable sales tax. Canadian residents will be charged applicable provincial taxes and GST. Offer not valid in Quebec. This offer is limited to one order per household. All orders subject to approval. Credit or debit balances in a customer's account(s) may be offset by any other outstanding balance owed by or to the customer. Please allow 4 to 6 weeks for delivery. Offer available while quantities last.

Your Privacy: Silhouette is committed to protecting your privacy. Our Privacy Policy is available online at www.eHarlequin.com or upon request from the Reader Service. From time to time we make our lists of customers available to reputable third parties who may have a product or service of interest to you. If you would prefer we not share your name and address, please check here. ☐

SRS08R

Silhouette *Desire*

Gifts from a Billionaire

JOAN HOHL

THE M.D.'S MISTRESS

Dr. Rebecca Jameson collapses from
exhaustion while working at a remote
African hospital. Fellow doctor Seth Andrews
ships her back to America so she can heal.
Rebecca is finally with the sexy surgeon
she's always loved. But would their affair
last longer than the week?

**Available September
wherever books are sold.**

Always Powerful, Passionate and Provocative.

Silhouette®
Romantic
SUSPENSE

COMING NEXT MONTH

#1527 NATURAL-BORN PROTECTOR—Carla Cassidy
Wild West Bodyguards
When Melody Thompson returns to her hometown to investigate her
sister's murder, she runs straight into a mysterious and intriguing neighbor,
ex-rancher-turned-bodyguard Hank Tyler. The killer comes for Melody,
and only Hank can keep her safe—but will their instant attraction put them
in even greater danger?

#1528 COLTON'S SECRET SERVICE—Marie Ferrarella
The Coltons: Family First
On a mission to protect a senator, Secret Service agent Nick Sheffield
tracks down a threatening message, only to discover Georgie Gradie
Colton. The rodeo-riding single mom insists on her innocence. Nick is
taken with the feisty redhead, and he must figure out if this woman is
conning him or if he can trust her and the passion they share....

#1529 INTIMATE ENEMY—Marilyn Pappano
A secret admirer turned stalker sends lawyer Jamie Munroe into hiding in
the least likely of places—the home of ex-lover Russ Calloway. Russ and
Jamie have a stormy history, but his code of honor won't let him stand idly
by while her life is in danger. Being so close again brings up emotions that
may be just as risky....

#1530 MERCENARY'S HONOR—Sharron McClellan
Running for her life in Colombia, reporter Fiona Macmillan needs
mercenary Angel Castillo's help. She has an incriminating tape of the
Colombian head of national security executing a woman, and the man will
kill to get it back. Now Fiona and Angel must learn to trust each other—
and resist giving in to passion—to escape with their lives.

SRSCNM0808